Children of Light

Heather Macauley

Cover design & collage by Heather Macauley
Background sky by William Schimmel

H.O.M.E. Publishing, LLC
P.O. Box 1422
Salt Lake City, UT 84110
(801) 461-9030

ISBN 0-9648093-3-8

Amelia said, "Timothy, I'm not exactly sure how all of this applies to us. I mean, we've been traveling through time and dimensions, and learning quantum physics, but I don't know that I understand the point. It's all very interesting, but what are we supposed to do with this information when we get home?"

"What you do with the information will be your choice," said Timothy. "Having the information will give you a choice."

INTRODUCTION

I remember as a little boy, I wanted so much to be able to think like a grownup. I figured that I'd be able to answer any question that ever came up, to solve any problem that ever came up, and to help anybody who needed help -- including those who needed help but didn't even know it! When things got difficult I'd ask myself, "How would I deal with this if I were grown, as an adult?" I became very serious as a child, even considered precocious, mature, and wise beyond my years.

When I was around seventeen I decided that I would no longer be in such a hurry to grow up, that adulthood seemed full of a lot more (and worse) problems and troubles than childhood, and that life certainly was already complicated enough just being seventeen. Still, I was very serious and everything was still so important. We were all supposed to be deciding what we wanted out of life and doing our (age-appropriate) best to start in that direction.

I remember my dreams changing. I could no longer fly, or run like the wind, or catch a falling star (to put in my pocket and save for a rainy day). I remember how rational thought took over in my dreams, while I tried to figure out what was going on all the time and what was the significance of it all. And, since I had already stopped praying in the wakeful state, there was no room for God in my dreams, I figured.

With adulthood came the witnessing of struggle and suffering and conflict and illness and death. With adulthood came parenting -- and the witnessing of innocence, and the miracles of life through birth, and the magic of a child's world. I found myself in the curious and ironic state of envy of such youthful innocence. I found myself fighting to somehow protect that magic as an inalienable right of childhood. Hopefully, other children would not wish to think like grownups too much and thus too-soon lose their youth.

In recent years, I have been able to rediscover magical, childlike thinking. It took what many would consider an extra-complicated route in order to return -- learning to let go of logic in the middle of a dream and just go with it; letting kids teach me how to play again; letting go of harsh judgments and the need to be right; releasing attachments to the way I had remembered things, learned things, taught stuff. Fun and faith and hope and more fun and knowing things will work out 'cause that's just what's gonna happen. "Hey, lighten up! Let's not take this stuff so seriously!   Come on -- we're all just kids, anyway!"

When we let the light back into our lives, we realize that we are all children of light. I am personally grateful to those masters of magic and light with whom I have orbited as mentors, colleagues, friends, playmates (Dr. Deepak Chopra, Prof. George Wald, Louise Hay, Mother Teresa, Brother Blue, Kermit the Frog -- just to name a few). I am honored to welcome a new master in Heather Macauley -- and I am glad to share in her magic and light.

Through my association with Dr. Chopra at our Center for Mind Body Medicine, I have had the privilege of reviewing many manuscripts and proposals for endorsement and support. I immediately became excited (like a kid!) upon experiencing **Children of Light**. This wonderful journey not only captures the principles of Vedic sciences, Quantum Mechanics, human psychology, spiritual traditions, and mind-body healing with accuracy and depth, it does so with enthralling and suspenseful entertainment which reaches audiences of practically any age. She is truly a gifted storyteller.

What does all this mean, anyway? While in the midst of grounding ourselves in the harshness of reality and practicality, along comes some creation of nature which gently--but powerfully--elevates our minds and spirits to higher states of awareness and possibility. We are returned to the realm of magic and of "me, too!" and of "Yes, I can!" For some precious time we are captured by the spirit of giving, of loving, of sharing, and teaching. We are floating -- flying -- transcending, above and beyond the bounds of the mundane of our existence, to experience a lightness of being -- as beings of light.

In this everyday world we perceive ourselves as distinct, separate beings, having totally separate existences and experiences from one another. Things happen, and they are seemingly done to us by others, causing us either grief or joy, failure or success, illness or health, pride or disgrace. We, thus, see ourselves as essentially alone, surrounded by billions of others who are also alone, but whose actions cause all of those situations with which we have to somehow cope. We are taught that mind and matter are completely separate and independent of one another, and that we are primarily physical things, cr eatures that have evolved into "thinking machines." Our presumptions are that the 'objective world' is the only true reality -- what really matters -- and that this existence of the universe is independent of our perception, participation, or lack thereof. Moreover, we are taught that intelligence and mind are finite limitations of the brain, the nervous system, and genetics.

Amazingly -- miraculously -- the consciousness of a child is not burdened with these constraints. It is the consciousness of true freedom, of magical beginnings, of magical being. It is through our socialization process that we succumb to such a different set of conclusions and core beliefs about universe and existence.

Through the contributions of our growing family of masters of literary magic, more and more of us are turning to that state of knowing greater truths. We are not self-contained entities totally independent of one another -- rather, we are inseparably connected as a set of cosmic relationships. Aloneness does not exist. Emotions and our responses to actions (reactions) are choices. Mind is unbounded, infinite, and can find expression in, though is not encased in physical structure. Matter exists because of consciousness -- not the other way around. Intelligence is infinite and universal. And it is as beings of light, of truth, of love -- as Children of Light -- that we know the magic of the master plan, our universal playground.

As we each read this story, may we all give to ourselves the permission to once again embrace the light....

Enrico Melson, MD, MPH, FACPM
Center for Mind Body Medicine
Del Mar, California
April, 1995

Dedication

This book is dedicated to all Star Children and especially to my sons, Ian and Andrew, who have blessed me with their loving, joyous presence and awakened me to all the children of the world.

TABLE OF CONTENTS

Children of Light

Chapter 1

Facing Death

How strange it was to be only sixteen and facing death. The tranquility of the desert night with its vast array of glittering stars and the merest crescent moon belied the imminent danger of hypothermia. There was little comfort in the fact that Amelia wouldn't be dying alone. She barely knew the boy sitting by her side. Matthew had been randomly chosen as her hiking partner by their geology teacher but they'd never really spoken until that day.

The hiking had been so beautiful. It was seventy degrees. The sky was clear and blue and so incredibly immense. They'd scrambled up and down over boulders gathering rock samples for their class. They hiked through fields of coarse grass, sage and prickly pear, and along dried stream beds. There was something about the desert that was peaceful yet exhilarating.

Deep, earthy colors contrasted vividly with the sky. Everything was on such a grand scale that Amelia hardly noticed the lack of trees and water. She'd always expected the desert to be flat and boring, yet in reality the desert canyons had endless variations.

They'd planned to head back sooner but Matthew was constantly being drawn around another bend or to the top of a plateau and would not rest until Amelia had shared the view. The beauty was more spectacular around each corner. This probably had something to do with the fact that the sun was slowly setting and the colors were deepening in the sky. As shadows lengthened across the canyon Amelia realized how late it was and convinced Matthew to turn back.

"Don't worry. We'll make it!" Matthew had sounded confident but Amelia noticed a certain urgency in his walk. They climbed through crevices and cracks in the rock that were hardly visible from just a few feet away. Even though they were hiking back on the same trail, it was barely recognizable when heading in the opposite direction. Wherever the land was fairly flat they ran instead of walked. As it grew darker, Matthew realized he'd forgotten to bring his glasses. He'd been wearing prescription sunglasses all day but with dusk settling in he could no longer see to lead the way.

Until this point Amelia had felt confident that Matthew would take care of everything but now it was up to her to get them back. She took the lead and tried to run from one rock cairn to the next but her body would no longer allow it. When they climbed steep cliffs she could feel the muscles in her legs shaking from exhaustion. She tried to jog through the fields but could manage no more than a fast walk.

In the shadow of the outcrops Amelia could barely see any markers. Several times they had to retrace their steps in order to find the next cairn. At last they climbed to the top of another plateau. There was just enough light to see the cairns up ahead and, despite exhaustion, Amelia tried to run as fast as she could from one to the next. They were so close and yet suddenly it was too dark to see any further. The sky had turned a soft sable and three stars twinkled around the crescent moon.

Under other circumstances it would have been serene and peaceful, but Amelia was gripped with fear. Her heart pounded in her chest and blackness made her too dizzy to walk straight. Finally, they sat down. Amelia tried to appear calm but she could feel her heart beating anxiously in her chest.

The temperature had been dropping quickly as the sun was setting and now it was quite cool. Amelia put on her sweater. It was warm and cozy and she immediately felt better. Silently they watched more stars appear as the moon sank slowly below the horizon. Amelia handed Matthew half of her sandwich.

"Thanks. I'm starving," he whispered.

She thought it was funny that here they were in the wilderness where even screaming and yelling wouldn't be heard, and yet it seemed only right to whisper. It was as if they felt the reverence and awe of being in the world's largest cathedral. Amelia looked up at the vast array of stars dangling like faintly tinted jewels.

"The constellations don't even look the same," she said. "They're so much brighter and bigger than anything I've ever seen. Do you see that really bright star?"

"No," said Matthew. "I can't see a thing without my glasses."

As Amelia peered into the darkness she had the strangest sensation looking at that star. She felt quite certain that it was flashing different colors: red, yellow, green, blue. Suddenly it dropped and then zigzagged. As she continued staring at it she began to feel as if she were looking down a long tunnel and it had become the only star in the sky. She felt light-headed and could barely sense her body. She sat in this near trance-like state with no sense of time.

Finally, Matthew said, "What about the star?" Amelia gasped slightly and her body jerked.

"I'm sorry," he said. "Did I scare you?"

Amelia took a deep breath. She shook her head a little and tried to regain some clarity. "I have the strangest feeling that's not really a star."

"Do you think it's a satellite?"

"No."

Matthew was quiet for a moment and then said, "What did you see?"

"It's not just what I'm seeing; it's how I feel when I look at it. It's been turning different colors and sort of bouncing around. I know that sounds weird. The strangest thing is that my body started feeling sort of light and tingly. And I didn't hear voices or anything, but I had this odd feeling someone was trying to talk to me -- not out loud, but trying to talk directly to my mind. I really can't explain it."

They sat in silence for a few minutes. "You know," said Matthew, "I think if someone from outer space offered to take me somewhere, I'd go."

"Really? What about your family? Wouldn't you worry about them?"

Matthew sat quietly for a moment, then said, "I know this sounds kind of cold, but I don't feel like I'm part of a family. It's more like I'm a statistic: Matthew James McKinley the third; first-born son; 4.0 grade average; possession of Matthew James McKinley the second and his lovely wife, Elizabeth.

"What are your parents like?"

Matthew picked up a rock and started scratching the surface of the boulder where they were sitting. "Have you ever been in a situation where everyone was doing and saying the right thing, but it just doesn't feel right?"

"Of course," said Amelia, "just pick a family holiday!" They laughed. It was an insight known by many but shared by few.

Matthew continued, "My parents despise each other but they've always maintained the 'we're-so-happy' look for outsiders, visiting dignitaries. And they at least try to be 'nice' in front of the children. I'm sure you've heard some version of this story before."

"I'm afraid so," said Amelia.

"And," he said, "in the midst of my parent's badly hidden, personal turmoil I've always felt invisible. So what's the difference if I left the planet on a friendly UFO? What do you think? Are we gonna get on this flight together?"

"Sounds good to me!" said Amelia.

"Why? What are your parents like?"

"Well, there's this Bible story where there was a very wise man named King Solomon. And when these two women came to him, both claiming to be the mother of the same baby, King Solomon said that the baby should be cut in half; whereupon the real mother told him to just give the baby to the other woman. King Solomon knew that the one who loved the baby enough to give it up had to be the real mother. Clever guy. Now, in my situation, my parents are getting divorced. I'm their only child and, unlike the baby in the story, they both *agreed* to just cut me in half, so no matter what I do one feels loved and the other feels hurt. I can't live with them both at the same time so if I didn't live here at all that would settle it!"

"What do your parents do?" said Matthew.

Amelia chuckled, "Are you ready for this?" she said. "They're both psychologists and Mom specializes in: Ta Da! Family Counseling! Honestly, Matthew, it's like the blind leading the blind."

Matthew quickly added, "Or 'physician, heal thyself'? No! Wait! 'Physicians, heal thyselves!'"

Amelia laughed. "That's *very* good. What about your parents?"

"Ah, yes. Well, my father is the 'great white hunter.' He retired at thirty after inheriting a *lot* of money. And now we have the heads of dead animals from India, Africa and South America hanging in his study. I detest the place. Mother plays the doormat role but she's one of those doormats that'll bite you in the rear if you're not careful!"

Amelia laughed. She was starting to get a feel for who Matthew was. At the same time, she realized she couldn't really remember exactly what he looked like. She knew he was about six feet tall with light brown, shoulder-length hair he wore pulled back in a pony tail. He had an athletic build like a mountain climber and he dressed simply in jeans and a flannel shirt.

Though she couldn't remember specific details about his face, she knew he had dark brown eyes, ruddy cheeks, and that he was basically attractive. She couldn't really remember if he were technically 'good looking' because who Matthew was inside was quite appealing and she knew that if she actually lived to see his face again that she'd find him to be handsome.

They sat quietly for a few moments and Amelia shuddered from the cold. She'd been so engrossed in the conversation and her own thoughts that she hadn't even noticed the quick drop in temperature. Her teeth began to chatter and the rock she was sitting on felt cold and hard.

"How cold is it going to get tonight?" said Amelia.

"It'll probably drop to below freezing. Do you know what that means?"

"What?"

"It means we could die from hypothermia."

It was quiet for a moment, then Amelia said, "Do you think they'll look for us?" She was frightened again. She wasn't about to admit it though. At that moment Matthew put his arm around her. Tears began to stream down her cheeks.

"I'm sure they'll look for us," he said, "but they'll be looking at Canyon Rim which is nowhere near here.

I'm sorry. It's my fault. I never should have taken you off the trail."

"It's okay," she said touching his hand lightly. "It was my choice too."

As they sat in silence Amelia thought about her life. Everything seemed so confusing. If she were just going to die, what was the point in living in the first place? She thought to herself, "I know this seems trivial, God, or whoever you are, but I've never been to the prom or homecoming or even on a real date for that matter! If I die now, is that fair?"

It was a poor excuse for a prayer but it was the best she could do under the circumstances. Amelia hadn't exactly been gliding through adolescence and as yet she hadn't decided who was to blame. Was it God, or genetics, or poor parental advice?

Amelia was taller than most boys her age. She had medium-length, dishwater-blonde hair that she tried to lighten in the summer with lemon juice and sunshine. Her eyes were an unusual blue-green color and though she wasn't unattractive her father kept telling her she'd grow into her looks. Until this year her breasts had been virtually nonexistent. When at last she was blessed with a little development in this department, she discovered to her dismay that she was no longer "one of the guys." Being a tomboy was familiar territory; being a woman was not.

Amelia had always been competitive with boys, not to mention the fact that she was in all the advanced placement classes and a straight 'A' student. Her grandmother was saying, "You know, dear, boys like to win. If you beat them at games, or if you act too smart, they won't take you out on dates. So let them win and don't say too much."

That concept grated against everything Amelia believed in. She decided right then and there that she would never let a boy win, nor would she play dumb. But then again, based on the fact that she'd never been on a real date, her grandmother might have been right after all.

It seemed funny that all these trivial things should be going through her mind when here she was facing death.

"Matthew, do you believe in God?"

"I don't know," he said. "We never went to church. What about you?"

"I'm not sure. I've heard so many versions of 'God' I don't know what to think. Do you think we're gonna die?"

Matthew hugged her and she started to cry again.

The night grew colder. The stars seemed more and more distant. Amelia's body began to shake uncontrollably. Matthew sat behind her with his chest against her back and put his arms around her. This helped a little, but she knew it was a losing battle. The coldness of the rock they were sitting on felt as if it had penetrated into her bones and was drawing out the little warmth she had left in her body.

Facing Death

Mostly she kept her eyes closed but when she did open them she always saw the bright star changing colors. She felt herself drifting in and out of consciousness and she couldn't figure out if it was the star or the cold that was having this effect on her. The next time she opened her eyes the star was much closer. She could tell that the flashing colors were on the base of what she could only assume was a starship.

She could see that the lights were set up in a circular pattern. There was a row of yellow, followed by green, then blue, then red and back to yellow again. The lights lit up in such a way that it followed this circular pattern. But when it was further away it had seemed like a single blinking light.

Amelia had heard of people seeing strange things in the desert. Was this an illusion brought on by the cold? Matthew couldn't see that far so there was no sense in asking him. She felt very light headed, as if she were about to float out of her body. Amelia thought, "This must be what it's like to die. This isn't so bad."

Suddenly, before them stood a golden-haired child, a little girl no more than ten or eleven years old. She had rosy cheeks and a wreath of wild flowers in her hair. She wore a simple white dress and had no shoes on her feet. She carried no light, and she certainly didn't glow from within, yet Amelia and Matthew could see her clearly. However, they still couldn't see each other.

The child smiled sweetly, "I'll take you both back to your camp." At that moment Amelia and Matthew could see everything. What had seemed a simple hike in the daytime could have proved fatal at night. There was only one path leading down and on either side of the path there were sheer cliffs.

Amelia was filled with questions but nothing came out of her mouth. Her body had the strangest feeling. She wasn't cold or stiff. She felt as if she were barely touching the ground. They walked quietly back to camp and before they could thank the child she turned to them and said, "Nobody knows you were missing, so just go to bed."

Amelia blurted out, "What do you mean, they don't know we're missing? They'd have to know we didn't make it back!"

The child continued as if she didn't hear Amelia. "In the morning everything will be the same and everything will be different." Immediately the child disappeared. Amelia couldn't find her voice. She just stood there staring at the place where the child had been. In the dim glow of the remaining camp fire she could see Matthew's face. He didn't seem the least bit puzzled or perturbed. He looked calm and peaceful. Matthew turned to Amelia, put his arms around her, gave her a big bear hug and said, "Goodnight." He then went to his tent.

As Amelia walked into her tent her mind was racing. She thought, "How could he just say goodnight as if nothing extraordinary had happened?" Without even undressing she crawled into her down sleeping bag. "How could that child have known that nobody was looking for us?" she thought. "How on earth did she find us? And what happened to her? Was she an extraterrestrial? If so, at least she could have admitted it." Questions flew through her mind but as she sank into the warmth and comfort of her sleeping bag her eyes closed involuntarily and she fell asleep.

Amelia awoke to find sunlight streaming into the tent. She yawned and stretched and remembered this strange dream she had the night before but, oddly enough, it didn't feel like a dream. Everything was so vivid that being awake felt more like a dream in comparison. She thought, "What was it that child said? 'Everything will be the same and everything will be different.'" She looked around at the other girls sleeping peacefully and thought, "Well everything certainly is the same. I don't see what's so different."

At that moment their instructor came to the tent to wake the girls up. "Rise and shine everybody!" The girls slowly started to wake up as Mrs. Caldwell rattled on about breakfast duty, who was to cook, who was to wash up. She looked right at Amelia and said, "Where's Amelia? Have you girls seen her?"

Amelia laughed. "Very funny. I'm sitting right here." All eyes turned toward Amelia's cot and the girls began talking at once.

"I haven't seen her since yesterday afternoon!"

"Didn't she go hiking with Matthew?"

"Has anybody seen him?"

All at once Amelia realized nobody could see her.

Chapter 11

Everything will be the same
and everything will be Different

She felt her heart beating and her breath becoming short. She tried yelling but there was no response. She reached out to grab one of her friends only to discover that she couldn't make contact. It was like trying to grab a holographic image. She couldn't make herself seen, heard or felt. Her stomach was in knots as adrenaline coursed through her veins.

Amelia hurried out of the tent trying to find anyone who might acknowledge her presence. She saw Matthew coming toward her. "Please, God," she thought, "let him see me."

Matthew waved his arms and cried, "Amelia!"

"Can you see me?" she cried. "No one else can!"

He rushed up to her and said, "No one can see me either!"

At this point, people began running through the camp frantically asking if anyone had seen Amelia and Matthew. Finally, one of the teachers started beating on a pot with a large, metal spoon and yelled, "Everyone! Gather over here." Matthew and Amelia tried desperately to be noticed but there was no response. Finally, they withdrew to a nearby hillside and watched helplessly as the teachers began to form search parties and made plans to contact forest rangers.

They sat in silence for a while and then Matthew asked, "Do you think this has anything to do with that little girl we saw last night?"

"I'm not sure. I can't figure it out." Amelia was quiet for a few moments. "How come you never said anything about her last night? You acted like everything was so ... normal."

"It's hard to explain," he said, "I felt like I was walking in a dream. One minute I was freezing to death in pitch darkness and the next minute I'm warm and I can see. I didn't even feel like I was walking; it was more like floating and I couldn't feel my body except for this tingly, warm feeling. When we reached the camp it just felt like everything was as it should be, like when you dream you're swimming under water and breathing and that seems perfectly normal and reasonable until you wake up and think, 'that's not possible.'"

Amelia stared at Matthew silently for a moment. "What if we're dead? I've read about people who've died and come back to life. They talk about being outside of their bodies but not being able to communicate with anyone and yet they still have bodies just like we do."

"Well," said Matthew, "if we're dead, then where did we leave our bodies?"

Amelia thought for a moment. "Maybe we really did die of hypothermia and that little girl was some sort of an angel. In that case, our bodies would be on the rocks where she found us."

Matthew grabbed Amelia's hand and said. "Let's go." They ran quickly and though it was a steep climb they found it to be quite effortless. They had no trouble finding the place where they'd been. There was a water bottle Amelia had accidentally left behind, but no bodies. They walked around, climbed back down the rock face and onto a dirt trail. Amelia was following Matthew and suddenly she stopped.

"Matthew! Look! We're not leaving any footprints!"

Matthew looked at the trail and then at Amelia. "My, God! We *must* be dead. But what happened to our bodies?"

A voice from behind them said quietly, "You're not dead."

They turned and saw the little girl, dressed the same as the night before.

"Well, what happened to us?" Amelia demanded.

"You're in another dimension," said the girl.

"What do you mean, another dimension?" said Matthew.

"It might be a little difficult to understand. Maybe we should sit down."

"Wait!" said Amelia, planting her feet and crossing her arms. "Who are you? Where did you come from?"

The little girl sighed. "There's so much to explain. Please, sit down." Amelia shifted back and forth uncomfortably for a few moments and then flopped to the ground frustrated and utterly confused. Matthew sat next to her and seemed to be taking things more in stride, which was a bit annoying in itself.

The girl sat facing them. She closed her eyes and took a few deep breaths. Amelia felt a sense of peace and well-being.

The girl opened her eyes. In her previous panic Amelia hadn't noticed the child's radiance. Her eyes were almost translucent and so intensely blue that Amelia found it difficult not to stare. The child looked directly into her eyes and held her gaze. Amelia had never felt so vulnerable, as if this child could see into her very soul, all of her deepest, darkest secrets. Yet there was no feeling of judgment. She felt as if she were staring into the eyes of mother and child at the same time; eyes both wise and innocent, sea and sky, jewels transposed with flowers. Amelia felt as if she were floating in the center of the universe surrounded by stars. There were no constellations that she could recognize and yet it all seemed so familiar. Her heart filled with joy and she began to dance among the stars; yet "dancing" is too earth-bound a concept for what she was able to do and feel.

Imagine the body "singing," or think of swimming in an ocean of pure light, glittering with an infinite spectrum of color beyond anything you've ever seen.

16

Colors as feelings, alive and distinct, yet blending together. A rainbow into white light, the spirit of Christmas, the dance of a first kiss.

Gradually, Amelia realized she hadn't moved. Her eyes had never closed and she'd remained fully conscious. It was like being in two places at once. She blinked, looked at Matthew, then back at the child. "Where was I?"

"Home," said the little girl.

"I've *never* felt like that at home."

"This isn't your home. You know, Einstein said 'Imagination is more important than knowledge.' You both need to use your imaginations for what I'm going to tell you. Forget what you *think* you know. Just *imagine*. Instead of judging what you see or hear as 'right' or 'wrong' simply say to yourselves, 'This is a possibility.' Are you both willing to stay open to possibilities?" Amelia and Matthew both nodded.

"My name is Äsha. I come from a star system called the Pleiades. It has seven stars known as the Seven Sisters but the Pleiades is actually comprised of several hundred stars."

"How long did it take you to get here?" said Amelia.

"No time at all. We can simply think of a destination and arrive."

"How's that possible?" said Matthew.

Everything will be different . . . .

"It's possible because I live in another dimensional reality. To understand this you must begin to see the enormity of creation and that life on Earth is really quite primitive. The earth in comparison to the Milky Way is smaller than a speck of dust; and the Milky Way in comparison to the universe would be about the size of an atom, not even visible to the human eye.

"If you think about it, life on Planet Earth has only *really* evolved in the last hundred years. Think of civilizations that have been evolving for trillions of years, beings that exist multi-dimensionally. Now, *think of the possibilities!* Imagine life as pure consciousness, that you don't wake up from dreams into reality, but you merely shift from one consciousness into another."

Amelia threw her arms up in the air and exclaimed, "Wait! Stop! Go back! What are you talking about? We live in a dream? Multi-dimensional? Who? What?"

Matthew said, "How do you shift consciousness?"

It was quiet for a moment. Then Amelia said skeptically, "You don't seem anything like a child to me."

"I'm not a child in the sense that you're thinking. It just seemed to me that this form would be the most acceptable and least frightening. Alright, I'll just tell you what I am."

Matthew and Amelia leaned forward anxiously as Äsha looked closely at them.

"No, you must understand other dimensions before I can explain about myself."

Children of Light

"Wait," said Amelia. "I don't mean to interrupt, but there are a lot of people looking for us right now and we really don't have time to talk about this. We need to let someone know we're alright."

Äsha was quiet. Amelia looked at her skeptically and said slowly, "That is, of course, unless we really are dead."

Chapter III

Missing from the Third Dimension

"You're not dead in the classical sense of the word. You are, however, 'missing' from the third dimension. Time as you know it is relative and in this dimension we can 'play' with time. And though you won't understand this now, you will be able to return and your friends' experience will seem to them to be only a hazy dream."

Amelia felt so completely confused and overwhelmed that she began to feel her logical mind just giving up. She could no longer force herself to make any sense of all that was happening.

"So why are we being held captive here?" said Matthew.

"You're not captives. Both of you actually agreed to this before you ever came here."

"What do you mean?" said Amelia, shaking her head. "No one ever said anything about this before our trip."

"No, I mean before you came here to the earth-plane."

"You're saying," said Matthew in utter disbelief, "that in my mother's womb I somehow agreed to be kidnaped into another dimension while on a high school field trip?"

"It is so difficult that you remember nothing. Though most people are quite unaware of this, you choose everything before you come to the earth. You choose your family, your name, your date of birth. You even have a plan for what you want to accomplish. Both of you chose to be on what you might call the accelerated program. And that's what this is all about.

"In *true* reality, not the reality that you know, life is pure consciousness. You know everything; you have total access to the Universal Intelligence. In fact, you're an integral part of it. Every experience and feeling is recorded. You come to the earth-plane or the third dimension for the purpose of learning. You're teachers and students at the same time."

"Why would we come here to learn, if we already know everything?" said Amelia.

"Imagine you were choosing between two doctors," said Äsha, "and you had the choice between a doctor who had read every book on surgery that had ever been published but had no experience; or a doctor who wasn't as well read but had twenty years experience as a successful surgeon. Who would you go to? Or imagine the difference between reading a romance novel about first-love, and how it actually feels to be in love. However, nothing ever happens against your will; it must still be your choice to learn. If you don't choose 'the accelerated program' I can take you both back to your camp and you'll return to the third dimension. But I must tell you that your decision will affect this entire planet."

"We're in high school!" exclaimed Matthew. "How much of a difference can we make?"

Äsha sat quietly for a moment and said, "Watch."

Before them appeared a holographic image. From a perspective high above they saw a chain of tropical islands in the South Pacific. As they watched, it was as if they were "floating" down to one particular island.

"Where is this?" said Amelia.

"The island of Koshima, near Japan, 1952," said Äsha. "You'll see monkeys being studied by a group of scientists."

As the holographic image brought them closer, they saw they were on a beach surrounded by lush, dense jungle. Before them was a pile of sweet potatoes and a colony of monkeys eyeing the potatoes suspiciously. Finally, one monkey picked up a potato and, after toying with it for a while, took a bite. The other monkeys also tried the potatoes and, although they seemed to find the flavor pleasant, they quite obviously found the dirt distasteful.

Amelia and Matthew laughed as they watched the different ways in which the monkeys tried to remove the dirt: brushing the potatoes with their hands or wiping them on themselves or each other. It never seemed to be quite good enough. Then they watched as a young female, about eighteen months old, took her potato to a nearby stream and washed it. As they watched, time began moving more quickly. They saw the monkey show her playmates and her mother this technique and her playmates in turn showed their mothers. They also noticed that the other adults refused to learn the method.

They watched time move rapidly through a six-year period. They saw a bird's-eye view of other colonies of the same monkey species on other islands in the chain and on the mainland, but none of those monkeys were washing their potatoes. Yet on the island of Koshima all the young monkeys grew up learning this washing technique. However, even after six years, the older monkeys still refused to adopt the procedure.

Then time slowed down to an autumn day in 1958. A particular young monkey in the colony was being taught to wash its potato. In that moment something happened. All the older monkeys who had never washed their potatoes before began washing them.

Then the holographic image shifted and showed them all of the colonies on all the islands and on the mainland. Almost all of the monkeys were adopting the new technique, and this was taking place on the very same day that this one last monkey was being taught to wash its potato. Then the image vanished.

"Did that really happen?" said Amelia.

"It did!" said Matthew. "I read about it. Scientists call the phenomena 'critical mass.' It's strange because it doesn't have anything to do with the habits or beliefs of the majority. It has something to do with *conscious* thought causing what's called a 'self-sustaining' chain reaction.

Missing from the third dimension

"What about the monkeys on the other islands?" said Amelia. "They never saw the young monkeys washing their potatoes. Why would they all suddenly start doing something they'd never seen before?"

"That's just it," said Matthew. "Scientists are starting to believe that we're all linked in some way. I guess you could say our minds are sort of like drops of water in a sea of consciousness. So, when people are making conscious choices and there are enough of them, there's a point where everyone who's, you know, on auto pilot, will find themselves doing things differently; the way a drop of dye would change the color of a glass of water."

"You may think that your choices couldn't possibly make a difference," said Äsha, "but notice how everything appeared to stay the same until just one more monkey learned. That one monkey caused the consciousness of all the monkeys to shift and the shift had nothing to do with experience or exposure. Don't underestimate what you can do. You never know if you might be the *one* who makes all the difference."

They all sat quietly for a few minutes. Then Äsha said, "So, would you like to continue learning or would you prefer to go back to your camp?"

Amelia said, "I'll stay."

She looked at Matthew. He smiled and said, "Me too."

His eyes twinkled as he raised his eyebrows and said, "It's the 'E' ticket, Amelia."

Children of Light

She laughed and noticed that Äsha looked a bit puzzled, so she said, "The 'E' ticket is for the best rides at Disneyland."

Suddenly Amelia saw in front of her an energy vortex. She closed her eyes and she could still see it. Intense neon shades of emerald green and amethyst swirled together with distinct patterns. It was like looking down into the eye of a hurricane with the shapes and colors of a kaleidoscope. She felt herself being drawn down the center of the vortex as if she were being pulled out of her body. Then she found herself surrounded by the most intense white light she had ever experienced. She immediately put her hands over her eyes but gradually took them away as she realized the light wasn't painful. She looked for the source of the light and when she looked down she realized that the light was emanating from her own body. Her body was pure, radiant light.

She saw she was standing in some type of an immense library, and there were others who were light also; each had varying hues and intensity and even different combinations of colors. Without knowing why, Amelia realized that she knew everything about each person she saw; but it was more than that. There was the feeling that she knew everything. She could comprehend past, present and future all at once; they were happening simultaneously.

In the library there were no books or computers, only disks of light. She reached out to touch one of the disks and the light from her body merged with the light on the disk; she instantly knew the contents of the disk.

Missing from the third dimension

Amelia could feel the light from her body radiating out with such intensity that it merged with all the light-disks in the library. She suddenly comprehended everything in the universe and saw that there was a perfect sense and order to everything.

Then a man came toward her. He was the most intensely luminous of all the people she'd seen. As his light touched her own she felt the most incredible sense of love. This love was powerful yet gentle, even harmless, and she felt as if she'd known him forever. Without words he communicated to Amelia that she was deeply loved and cared for and that when she returned to her physical body she wouldn't be able to remember all that she currently knew and felt.

Amelia's body jerked. She opened her eyes and saw Matthew staring at her. Amelia's breathing was at first uneven but eventually she became more calm and her breathing stabilized. Amelia looked at him for a moment and then turned to Äsha.

"You're light, aren't you? You're pure light! That's what you really are!"

Äsha smiled and nodded.

Excited, Amelia turned to Matthew. She explained some of what happened and then said, "For just a few minutes, I knew everything! *Everything!* It was just like Äsha said!"

Matthew leaned toward her and said, "Tell me!"

"I can't tell you what I knew; but I know I knew everything. And everything made perfect sense. It wasn't just what I knew, but how I felt. It's like, I was me and

I had a body, but it wasn't solid. I was pure light, but I was still myself."

Amelia stopped for a moment, feeling somewhat exasperated by her inability to describe her experience, finding that words were totally inadequate.

"Can you remember anything else?" said Matthew

"I can tell you one thing," said Amelia. "Time isn't the way we think it is. It's not linear; time doesn't go from point A to point B. It's more like the past and future are actually like different dimensions of the present."

"Come back." said Matthew. "Since I wasn't there you'll have to be patient with me."

"Sorry," said Amelia. "It's not like school where you're given facts and statistics. Instead, information comes like a feeling. You *feel* information instead of thinking information. I'm not actually sure I can describe this."

"Don't give up," said Matthew. "I'm almost with you. It's just a brand new concept."

"Well," Amelia continued, "think of a three-layered chess board. Imagine the 'past' as the bottom level, the 'present' as the middle, and on top is the 'future.' All the levels are transparent. So if you're looking down from the top you'd see everything all at once. Whatever shifts on the second level (or in the 'present') affects both the future and the past. In fact, changes in our future can affect the present."

Missing from the third dimension

"Wait! How could the present affect the past?" said Matthew. "The past is past. It can't change. And the future hasn't happened so it can't affect the present."

"I can't explain why it works that way," said Amelia, "but it does. The past isn't 'dead and gone' like we think it is; it isn't . . . solid." Amelia stopped. "This is impossible to explain. Äsha, will you try?"

Äsha looked at her affectionately and said, "Attempting to explain this will help solidify the ideas in your own mind. As you teach, you learn; just do your best."

Amelia searched for an image to describe what she'd felt. Then she had the strangest feeling she was getting help. It felt as if images were being projected into her mind. She took a deep breath and said, "Okay, Matthew, this is the closest I can get. Imagine the present as if it were liquid, like a river that's flowing, and the past as if it were frozen. The future's like moisture in the air; it's present but you're not aware of it. Wait! Better yet, imagine a man who's been frozen through cryogenics. He could stay in that state for hundreds or thousands of years, but if someone finds him and has the technology to bring him back to life then what's happening in the present is affecting the past and the future all at the same time."

Amelia stopped to see if Matthew understood. He smiled and said, "I'm with you so far."

"Now here's the hard part," she said. "Try not to be too analytical or you won't get it. What makes history change -- from being 'solid ice' to 'liquid' -- is a *conscious* decision in the present. The cryogenic man, or the 'past,' could've stayed frozen indefinitely, but the scientist, who represents the 'present,' would've had to make a choice about bringing the man back to life. In the same way we can consciously choose to bring the past back to life, so to speak, and change history simply by what we're thinking in the present about the past."

Matthew sat quietly for a few moments and then said, "So how can the nonexistent future affect the present?"

"Well," said Amelia, "to the cryogenic man, our present was his future. He wouldn't be waking up to *his* concept of 'present'; he'd be waking up in his 'future,' which would indelibly shape his sense of the present."

"Now, I'll tell you both a secret about how to change what you call the future," said Äsha. "There is *no* future. There's only **now**. Think about it. Can you grasp the future or the past? There really's only this moment. What you feel in this moment is what will create your so-called future experiences. Your feelings, not so much your analytical thought, literally magnetize to you your experiences."

"I think I'll have to stay with this one for a while," said Matthew.

"Remember," said Äsha, "you cannot perceive other dimensional reality from your analytical mind; just allow the information to flow through the imagination. Don't try so hard."

Missing from the third dimension

"I think it would be much easier," said Matthew, "if I could just go to some spinning energy vortex of my own. How come these things happen to Amelia and not me?"

"For one thing, try not to compare your experience to Amelia's. Everyone has unique life lessons tailored for whatever they're here to learn, and it's the same in this case too. Whatever you're ready for will come to you in a form that you can perceive without feeling threatened."

"What you do mean," said Matthew, "'without feeling threatened'?"

"Suppose," said Äsha, "that you were someone who loved snakes."

"Oh, I *hate* snakes!" said Matthew.

"But if you did love snakes and were extremely knowledgeable, not the least bit afraid, it wouldn't bother you if a friend handed you a snake or dropped one in your lap. You might even let the snake wrap itself around your neck or let its tongue brush your cheek."

"Yuck!" said Matthew, wincing.

"Now, Matthew, think of how you feel about snakes. Would you want someone to drape a snake over your shoulders?"

"I'd probably pass out."

"In the same way," said Äsha, "there are certain experiences that could be so frightening to you it would be impossible to learn because you'd have so much difficulty overcoming your fear. Amelia has the feeling of 'leaving' her body. She's able to go with it, but some people find the experience genuinely frightening, thinking that they may never be able to get back into their bodies. Or they may be holding some fear that closes them off from the experience. So, just keep in mind that whatever comes to you is perfect and when you're ready for more I promise you it will be there."

Äsha stood up and said, "I think we need a change of scenery."

Instantly they traveled through space and time, yet there was no sensation of movement. It was as simple as a scene change at the movies. They were all standing on a mountainside overlooking the Pacific, surrounded by wild flowers. The glittering ocean below peeked through the trunks of ancient sequoias. Azure blue canvassed fluffy, white clouds, drifting lazily across the sky, teasing the imagination with ever-changing pictures.

Chapter IV

Beyond the 'E' Ticket

"Whoa!" said Matthew, "I take it back! This is way beyond the 'E' ticket!"

"How did you do that!?" exclaimed Amelia.

"We're in another dimension," said Äsha. "The laws and limitations you know in the third dimension don't exist here. In this dimension, whatever you think becomes reality instantly."

"But I didn't think of coming here," said Amelia.

"That's true," said Äsha, "but you did agree to 'come along for the ride' and *this* is where the 'E' ticket brought you!"

Amelia laughed and shook her head, "This is totally beyond me."

"Let me begin by explaining the dimensions," said Äsha. "As you know, the first dimension could be represented by a dot on a piece of paper, and the second dimension would be a line; and of course you know that most of what comprises your world is in the third dimension.

"Now there are many dimensions beyond the third, but they're difficult to describe. For instance, if you were a two dimensional line on a piece of paper and you became a person for a day and then had to go back to being a line, you'd have a really difficult time describing to the other lines what it was like being a human and living in the third dimension. You see, there's no frame of reference. The same difficulty exists for you in your ability to comprehend dimensions beyond the third; this includes the concept of past, present and future as one.

"Amelia, your consciousness is very open, which is why you've been 'leaving' your body and having the feeling of being in two places at once. Your mind is able to release and have experiences of other dimensions. In your case, Matthew, having these experiences may not seem to come as easily to you because your thought is very linear and analytical."

"So where are we?" said Matthew.

"Right now, you're in the fourth dimension."

"Which means?" said Matthew.

"It means that you don't have the same limitations you had in the third dimension. There's no time or space or solid matter in this dimension. What you see are thought forms. Things are thoughts."

"Things are thoughts?" asked Matthew. "I don't get it."

"What has more substance, a chair or the idea of a chair?" said Äsha.

"A chair, of course," he said laughing. "You can't exactly sit on an idea!"

Äsha laughed, "That's one way of looking at it. However, you could destroy every chair that was ever made; could you destroy the idea of a chair?"

"No."

"So what is more substantial; the idea or the thing?"

Matthew thought for a moment. "I guess it would have to be the idea."

"So, anything you see began as an idea. That's why things are thoughts," said Äsha.

"Does this tie in with the question, 'Which came first, the chicken or the egg?'" asked Amelia.

"Well, since everything's in consciousness, there's no separation between the chicken and the egg," said Äsha. "The idea is one. Ideas don't have to start as infantile or mature. They can incorporate everything all at once."

"Where do the ideas come from?" asked Matthew.

"Where do you think intelligence comes from?" replied Äsha.

"My brain, I guess."

"Then what's the intelligence that told your body to develop from a few cells into a full body, complete with the brain that you think gives you your intelligence?"

"I don't know," said Matthew.

"Look at the life-force on this planet. Can't you see there's incredible, creative Intelligence all around you?"

She paused for a moment and then said, "There exists a Source of all intelligence, all love, and it's infinitely creative. Think of the sun as the source and the rays as the expression; you can't separate the sun from the rays. So everything you see, feel and experience around you is the expression of the Source, including yourselves. You can't separate the thought from the thinker."

"But where does this 'Source' come from?" asked Amelia.

"It just is," said Äsha. "Think of the origins of Love; the essence, the idea of Universal Love. Can you imagine this Love beginning or ending?"

"Then why do people hate each other?" said Amelia.

"Because they have the freedom of choice. They can choose not to express love, but they cannot choose the existence of Love."

"There's one thing I don't get," said Amelia. "You said that 'things are thoughts' and I understand the concept of the idea being more substantial than the thing, but I'm solid; the ground I'm standing on is solid."

"Are you sure?"

"Of course I'm sure!" said Amelia as she stomped her foot on the ground and squeezed her own arm. "I can feel that!"

"What if this is a dream you're having? Could you squeeze your arm and feel it, or stamp your foot on the ground?"

"Of course."

Äsha looked steadily into Amelia's eyes, "Then where is the ground in your dream? And what is it that's being pinched?"

Amelia thought for a moment, "Well, I guess it's in my mind."

"Does everything seem real to you when you're dreaming?"

"Most of the time."

"So how do you know you're not dreaming right now?"

Matthew and Amelia looked at each other and then back at Äsha. "Well, for one thing," said Amelia, "this doesn't feel like a dream."

"What does a dream feel like?"

"I don't know. More hazy and distant, I guess."

"Is it hazy and distant when you're having the dream, or does it seem real at the time?"

Amelia shook her head, shrugged her shoulders and said, "Well, I guess so. I mean, yeah, it does seem real."

"When you wake up you look at the dream and think, 'Oh, that was a dream; this is reality.' But what do you compare 'reality' with? How do you know what's 'real'?"

Amelia had never thought of questioning reality.

"You all look to each other and agree the world you live in is real," said Äsha, "but what if you're all in the same 'dream' together? You think nothing of creating entire worlds in your mind while you're dreaming, all kinds of people and events, yet you never question the world you wake up to.

"How often have you had dreams that, upon waking, made absolutely no sense, but you never questioned the 'reality' of it while you were dreaming? Does it make sense that people would destroy their own living environment? Or destroy their own families through physical and emotional abuse? The reason you never question your 'reality' is because you are so deeply immersed in the dream."

"Are you saying," asked Matthew, "that we spend our entire lives going back and forth between dream states, without ever waking up?"

"For the most part, yes. You could say that you simply *shift* from a sleeping-dream into a waking-dream, unless of course you consciously choose to 'wake up.'"

"How do you wake up?" asked Amelia.

"By being conscious of true reality," said Äsha.

"If we have no means of comparison then how do we know whether reality is true or not?"

"That's what you're here to learn and discover. Be patient. There's no quick answer to that one."

Matthew said, "I don't know if this exactly relates to what you're talking about, but scientists discovered that if a person is dreaming, for instance, they're sitting in a wheelchair, paralyzed, and they briefly wake up to discover they're fine, the person could then resume dreaming, still sitting in the wheelchair, but they'd no longer be paralyzed. Is that sort of like 'waking up,' because they realized what was true?"

"That's it exactly, but it's more than just knowledge; it's a feeling. Think of how it would be if you found you were paralyzed and how relieved you'd feel when you woke up. It wouldn't be just intellectual; you'd feel it physically and emotionally too. It's the *feeling* that would change the dream state. In the same way, it's not what's happening that determines your experience; it's how you *choose to feel* about what's happening."

"How can you choose what to feel?" said Amelia. "Things happen and you feel how you feel."

"Initially that's true," said Äsha. "You may react to a situation with anger or fear. But what if you asked yourself whether there was another way of looking at the situation?"

"How could you look at it differently?" said Matthew. "You can't change what happened."

"If you had a thousand people who all had the same experience, would they see it exactly the same way?" asked Äsha.

"I doubt it."

"So you could say that each person's experience is determined by their perception or their interpretation. And how you're perceiving something comes from the judgments you've made based on your past experience, what you've decided is good or bad, right or wrong. In other words, you can't change the experience but you can change your interpretation of the experience."

"I think you've lost me," said Amelia.

Suddenly, Amelia, Matthew and Äsha were all standing on a lake front beach where Amelia's family had a cabin. Amelia loved this place. Emerald Lake had the color and clarity for which it had been named. The scent of pine permeated the air, overpowering even the pungent odor of seaweed and fish that usually transpired from the soggy beach. Amelia looked around and was shocked to see herself from a year earlier standing on the dock on a hot summer evening.

They'd gone back through time!

The strangest thing was that Amelia could feel exactly how she'd felt that day. Her young cousin, Gerand, had been driving her nuts with his practical jokes: rubber dog poop, snakes, and spiders, live frogs and toads. It was a beastly hot, humid day but her parents had insisted she take her cousin on a nature hike. For lunch he'd made her a sandwich with anchovies, peanut butter, guacamole, potato chips, Tabasco sauce, mustard, mayonnaise and pickles. Unfortunately, she couldn't take his sandwich and force him to eat hers because he was eating the same thing.

As Amelia watched herself standing on the dock she noticed what appeared to be an energy field around her body. The energy extended out from her body about six to eight inches and was sort of a muddy, red color. It was as if she could see her own feelings in the color. She felt hot, tired and annoyed with her little cousin.

Amelia continued watching. She saw her past-self as she glanced over the edge of the dock and noticed something floating below her. As she leaned over to get a better look she was shoved into the water. Enraged, feeling this was absolutely the last straw, Amelia pushed off the bottom and was already making plans to kill her little cousin. But when she surfaced she was surprised to see her neighbor, Jordan, grinning broadly at her. He was tall and handsome; something between Prince Charming and the older brother she never had. She'd had a crush on him for years.

"Sorry, 'Melie! It was just too much of a temptation! Here, let me help you up," he said as he reached over the edge.

"That's okay! I needed to cool off!" She grasped his hand tightly and wedged her foot just below the dock. Then she pulled with all her might.

Jordan flew head first into the water. He burst to the surface, laughing heartily. They played and tickled and dunked each other until finally they walked back to the cabin tired and dripping, but happy. Amelia noticed that the muddy red color she had seen around herself had been replaced by a soft pink glow. How odd it was to have been standing in her own past, not remembering but experiencing her past in the present.

Amelia turned to Äsha and said, "Why did you show that to me?"

"In order to give you the opportunity to see, feel, and experience perception," said Äsha.

"What do you mean?"

"How did you feel at first when you were pushed into the water?"

"I was angry."

"Then what happened?"

"It turned out to be Jordan, my neighbor."

"Were you still angry?"

"No. I thought it was funny!"

"So let me ask you this: What changed? You went from angry to happy, maybe even a little ecstatic, in a matter of seconds."

"Well, the difference is that it wasn't my annoying little cousin."

"But the experience of being pushed in the water didn't change. So what changed? I'll give you a hint. Shakespeare said, 'Nothing is either right or wrong, but *thinking* makes it so.'"

Amelia still seemed lost.

"Let's put it this way. Could you have chosen to change your mind about your cousin if you'd wanted to?"

"Yes. But I didn't want to."

"Who were you making unhappy?"

Amelia thought back to her cousin. She hadn't really been paying attention at the time but now she realized she'd been able to feel his feelings too. He was having fun. The more he made her angry the better he felt.

"But what he did wasn't right," said Amelia.

"In other words, he was wrong and you were right."

"That's exactly it!" said Amelia, relieved that Äsha was finally seeing her point of view.

Äsha paused for a moment and said, "Okay, would you rather be right, or would you rather be happy?"

Amelia struggled with that for a few moments and said, "Well, can't I be both?"

"Part of being 'right' meant you were angry. Can you be happy and angry at the same time or do you have to choose?"

"Well, yeah, I'd rather be happy. But I'm not responsible for what my cousin was doing to me that day, or that he was making me angry."

"Let's look at the word 'responsible.' If we take it apart it means 'the ability to respond.' One meaning of 'respond' is 'to react positively, cooperatively.' In terms of your cousin, did you have the ability to respond positively if you'd chosen to?"

"Well, yeah, I could have."

"Look at it this way. If you'd rather be right than happy, you'll make other people responsible for your happiness. And, based on results, that doesn't work too well."

Amelia laughed, "True."

"But if you'd rather be happy, then you're the one responsible for your happiness. You're the one able to react positively. No one else is going to do it for you. It's always your choice. So did your cousin 'make' you angry or did you 'choose' anger instead of a positive reaction?"

"Got it," said Amelia. "It was my choice."

"Amelia, here's my last question on the subject. Could you have chosen a positive response to being pushed in the water, regardless of who pushed you?"

"Of course."

"Good! Let's move on. Are you with us, Matthew?"

"Absolutely!" said Matthew.

"Are there any questions?"

"I have one," said Matthew. "Why am I seeing colors around Amelia?"

Surprised, Amelia exclaimed, "When the 'past-me' was on the dock, you could see that too?!"

"Could?" said Matthew. "I still can! I've been sitting here watching the colors shift and change around you. When you're confused the color looks kind of muddy and brownish and when you begin to understand the color becomes more clear; the muddiness goes away."

"How come I can't see that around Matthew?" Amelia demanded.

"You each have your own talents. Amelia, you skip around in other dimensions and Matthew has the ability to see auras. The idea is cooperation, not competition."

Chapter V

The Field of Possibilities

Suddenly they found themselves standing next to an American man in his late forties, sporting glasses and wearing conservative yet disheveled clothing. He had a hat in one hand and a soggy handkerchief in the other which he used to mop his sweaty brow. Though they were in a room full of people, no one seemed to notice their sudden appearance except the Indian yogi to whom the American man was speaking.

The yogi sat with bare feet and crossed legs. He wore a white robe and turban. Though the surroundings were simple, Amelia had the feeling this man was powerful and important. He looked right at them and smiled slightly but didn't say a word.

"Where are we?" whispered Amelia.

"India, 1954."

Matthew said, "Don't they see us?"

"No, just the yogi. He's been trained to see multi-dimensionally. Now, just watch."

There was such a stark contrast between the yogi and the American, and not just in the way they dressed. Amelia noticed she'd become sensitive to the energy field surrounding each person. The feeling around the yogi was like the ocean on a calm, sunny day -- peaceful yet powerful at the same time. But the feeling around the American was sort of a combination: people rushing around after work in a major city and the uncomfortable feeling of waiting in a long line when you're in a hurry. Amelia thought it was odd she'd never really noticed this in people before and yet the feelings came so clearly and easily now that she was finally paying attention.

The American said, "Sir, as I said, I'm a psychiatrist from the United States. I'm the head Professor of Psychiatry at Stanford University. I understand that you're considered the best hypnotist in India and I'd like to try an experiment. I propose to challenge your ability in some form of a contest and I'd be willing to pay for this opportunity."

The yogi sat quietly for a moment. "There is a cave outside of the town. This boy," he said, indicating a child about eight years old, "will take you there. Meet me at the cave tomorrow morning at dawn. Your challenge will be simply to walk all of the way into the cave and walk back out."

"Thank you, sir," said the American, bobbing ineptly as he departed.

Äsha, Matthew and Amelia followed as the boy led the man toward the cave. They walked through the dusty streets of the small town. It seemed to be a place where very little changed, yet Amelia felt drawn to its simplicity. Though she didn't know any foreign languages, she was surprised when she realized she could understand everything that was being said around her. Still no one could see them, but Amelia noticed that animals were aware of their presence. This made her wonder what her own animals might have been "seeing" when they were reacting strangely to something that supposedly wasn't there.

They walked through the town until they reached a dirt road leading up into the hills. Then they continued on for another mile and took a narrow trail up a steep incline. The sun beat down on the dry grass and coarse, rangy shrubs. Amelia could see how hot it was by the perspiration streaming down the psychiatrist's face but, oddly enough, she felt perfectly comfortable. Finally, they reached the cave. The man tipped the boy and thanked him. The boy then turned and ran down the path.

The man pulled a small flashlight out of his bag and said to himself, "Always handy." He then stepped into the cave, still totally unaware he was being followed. He walked along the sandy-bottomed cave until he reached the back, shining his light on all of the walls. The cave wasn't even big enough to be pitch black. He looked around, shook his head and said, "Hmm, nothing." Then he turned, walked out, and headed back down the trail.

Äsha stood with Matthew and Amelia outside the cave.

"Well, now what do we do?" said Matthew. "Wait 'til morning?"

"We'll just speed up the process. Both of you, imagine yourselves here tomorrow at dawn."

The Field of Possibilities

Instantly everything changed except the place where they were standing. Gold and red streaks glistened across the sky as the dawn broke. Amelia smiled as she saw jewels of morning dew suspended on a nearly transparent spider's web. She'd never heard such a symphony of sounds. Songbirds trilled to a chorus of crickets, cicadas and other insects. And from the midst of all that came the occasional loud and high-pitched protest of a few territorial squirrels not too thrilled by the presence of humans.

Amelia was surprised to see not only how many people had gathered for this event, but that they were all sitting so quietly. It appeared that the entire town had gathered for the competition. The yogi was sitting about 20 feet from the mouth of the cave with the townspeople behind him and on both sides. Just as the sun fully appeared, the American reached the top of the trail. Rather out of breath, he acknowledged the yogi, turned toward the cave and instantly stopped dead.

At first Amelia and Matthew thought he could see them, but then they realized his focus was behind them. They turned and saw that the mouth of the cave had been totally sealed off with huge boulders and stones, impossible for any man to move alone. They watched as the man walked up and touched the boulders. He tried to move them but couldn't. He stopped and thought for a moment, then he said, "Oh, of course, it's not real." He then proceeded to ram into the boulders with his shoulder only to end up bruised and bloody. He jumped around in pain for a few minutes and finally sat on the ground, glaring angrily at the boulders.

Children of Light

Amelia turned to Äsha and said, "What's he doing wrong?"

"By physically trying to force his way in, he's giving his mental power over to the illusion. You see, he's *believing* there's an obstacle he needs to get past instead of recognizing it's only a mental picture. It's no different than the movies. The projector projects light onto a screen and creates images. What you see on the screen is actually nothing more than a play of light. Yet your mind translates these flickering lights into images that affect you physically and emotionally. And the depth to which you are affected is dependent solely on how much you believe what you see. This is called 'suspension of disbelief,' which means that for the time being the audience chooses to believe that what it sees and hears is real. But if someone in the audience closed their eyes, put on a headset and listened to music, or got up and walked out, their 'reality' would change instantly.

"In this case, the yogi is like the movie projector and the psychiatrist is the blank movie screen. The yogi is using his mind to project images into the mind of the psychiatrist and as long as the psychiatrist remains 'in the dark,' so to speak, he will continue believing what he sees. Now, think of what happens when you're watching a movie. Suddenly all of the lights come on and it's so brightly lit you can hardly see the screen? The 'reality' disappears instantly, doesn't it? So, think in terms of darkness as ignorance and light as knowledge. The psychiatrist simply needs to *know* that what he's seeing is nothing more than a false projection."

The Field of Possibilities

"But he's a psychiatrist," said Matthew. "Doesn't he know all of that already?"

"To know something mentally is not the same as having the experience. One thing the professor didn't expect to be dealing with is his own fear. His arm is bruised and bloody and he's feeling a great deal of pain judging from the look on his face."

"Well, how's that possible," said Amelia, "if it's not real?"

"Don't underestimate the power of belief, Amelia. That man's belief that he's been harmed by something real is more powerful than the fact that there's nothing there. Right now, he's afraid to try again. Now both of you, remember this: Fear stands for 'False Evidence Appearing Real.'"

"But wait a minute," said Matthew. "Aren't there some things you *should* be afraid of?"

"No. Fear is an indication that you are giving your power to an illusion. In reality there's nothing to fear."

"But I'd be afraid to drink poison," said Amelia.

"Then don't drink it."

"But you just said that we shouldn't be afraid."

"Actually, I said, 'There's nothing to fear.' It's never necessary to be afraid. However, if you are afraid and cannot overcome the fear then you need to honor your feelings until your belief changes."

Äsha was quiet for a moment. "Matthew, what are you seeing around that man?"

Matthew concentrated for a moment and said, "There's an energy field that's close to his body. It's a deep maroon color with bits of black; he's much angrier than he appears to be."

* * *

"Do you give up?" said the yogi loudly.

"No," said the professor, "I'm just thinking."

The yogi interpreted this statement for the audience and they all laughed, finding the situation quite amusing.

"Let's help him," said Äsha.

At that, the yogi looked directly at her. She smiled and waved and said to the yogi a bit loudly, "He does need some assistance."

"It will be much more powerful if we all do this together," said Äsha. "Imagine projecting 'light' into the man's consciousness. As you do this, simply keep in mind that what he's seeing is an illusion and remember what the cave really looks like."

As they did this, the man jumped to his feet. He walked up to the boulders, closed his eyes, took a deep breath and walked right through the stone wall. As he opened his eyes to look back at the wall, he watched it disappear. "Ha!" he exclaimed, getting his flashlight out of his pocket as he continued walking through the cave. Once again he was unaware that he was being followed.

The Field of Possibilities

Suddenly they came to a huge chasm, at least 15 feet across. He shined the light down into it but could see nothing. Then he threw a rock and they waited several seconds before they faintly heard it hit the bottom.

Amelia said, "I don't remember this being here."

"It's not," said Äsha.

"Oh, of course," said Amelia. "Should we help him out again?"

"Let's just watch this time . . . see if he figures it out himself. Of course the beauty of it is that he thinks he figured it out himself the first time, too!"

Sure enough, the professor took another deep breath, closed his eyes and walked across the "chasm." Once again he looked back and watched it disappear. They followed as he walked quickly around a corner and then abruptly came to a halt. There in front of him two cobras had reared up and were ready to strike. He laughed a bit nervously, took another deep breath, closed his eyes and walked right between them.

With his eyes closed he didn't even notice as the cobras tried to strike, nor did he see the cobras hit an invisible wall of energy and slump to the ground. This time the professor didn't bother to turn and see whether the "illusion" was still there, but continued walking briskly to the end of the cave. They watched as the slightly dazed cobras made their way to the walls and disappeared into the crevices. The psychiatrist then turned and walked jubilantly out of the cave.

"I don't get it!" exclaimed Matthew. "Those were *real* cobras! How did he do that?"

"His belief that the snakes were an illusion was more powerful than the so-called reality and this conviction literally set up an energetic force-field which the snakes couldn't penetrate."

"What if he'd been afraid that they were real, and still tried to walk past?" said Matthew.

"He would have been bitten. But notice: at first, he did think the cobras were real. Then he changed his mind about what he was seeing. It was that shift in his conscious thought that changed the 'reality,' making it impossible for the snakes to attack."

They walked out of the cave into warm sunshine. Amelia noticed the psychiatrist talking to the yogi. Then she said, "Look! His arm isn't bruised or bleeding anymore? That's impossible!"

"Have you heard the term, 'As above, so below'?"

"No," said Amelia.

"It means that whatever you believe in your conscious mind goes into the subconscious and is then out-pictured as your reality. This was once described as the subconscious being fertile soil and the conscious thoughts and feelings being the seeds. Whatever you're thinking and feeling is 'planted' in the subconscious. And these thoughts and feelings grow into your experience . . . which will be positive or negative, depending on what you're thinking and feeling.

"Your mind is literally a field of possibilities; whatever you hold to be true you will create. And, in the same way, you will never create an experience of something you don't believe or feel to be true. For the psychiatrist, he thought and literally felt what he believed when he rammed into the boulders. When he recognized it was an illusion and overcame his fear, the boulders became illusions. And, since he obviously doesn't believe he can be harmed by an illusion, the 'evidence' disappeared. Now, come listen to what he's saying."

They walked over to the man and watched as he talked with great animation to the yogi. He said, "You know, the only reason I got through that was because I came here yesterday. I saw the cave for myself. I knew there were no boulders or chasms or cobras . . . ."

"You saw cobras?" said the yogi. "Ah, how interesting."

"Yes. Well, like I was saying," the psychiatrist continued, "it was the memory of what the cave really looked like that helped me to recognize that everything else was just a hypnotic illusion."

"Keep that in mind," said Äsha. "When you focus on reality you can recognize the illusion or waking-dream and walk right through it."

"When I was younger," said Amelia, "I had trouble with nightmares. My parents, who are psychologists, taught me how to sort of 'wake-up' in my dream. So when this monster was chasing me I'd tell it to turn into a piece of cheese. And it did instantly. Once I knew I could do that, I wasn't afraid anymore and it didn't take long for the nightmares to stop."

"If you have a clear, conscious desire, *without fear*," said Äsha, "that's an important point. It *must* show up in your experience."

"But wait a minute," said Matthew. "One year I really wanted a bike for Christmas, more than anything, but I didn't get it."

"Were you afraid that you might not get it?"

"I guess so. My parents thought the bike I had was good enough, but I wanted a racing bike."

"Then your belief that you wouldn't get the bike was stronger than your belief that you would."

"Well, how do you know that?"

"Look at the results. Did you finally get a bike?"

"I got a paper route and saved up for it."

"Now think about how you felt. Did you 'hope' you were getting a bike or did you 'know' you were getting a bike?"

"Oh, I *knew* I was getting a bike. I picked it out before I'd even earned the money."

"Did you feel different from the time you were hoping for the bike at Christmas?"

"It was completely different. I wasn't depending on my parents. I made it happen myself."

"You see, Matthew, when you knew you were going to do it yourself, you weren't afraid of being disappointed. It may appear that the circumstances were different, but your perception had changed. Since there was no fear, your desire became a reality. So, if you want something to happen, remember the difference between the feeling of 'hoping' and the feeling of 'knowing' that it will happen."

"I'm not sure I totally understand," said Matthew.

"Think of the definition of those words. To 'hope' means you have 'some confidence' in the outcome. But to 'know' an outcome means you already see it as a fact. Can you see how the feeling of knowing, or certainty, would out-power the feeling of 'some confidence'? Remember, things are thoughts. What you believe is what you see."

* * *

"You have succeeded admirably, my friend," said the yogi, "but how would you feel if I told you that the cobras were not part of the illusion, that they were real?"

Instantly the color drained out of the psychiatrist's face and he looked like he was about to faint.

"Well that should give him something to think about," said Äsha. "Matthew, what did you see around him?"

"When he first came out of the cave his energy field was broad, going out maybe 12 inches from his body, and it was a bright yellow. As he talked I noticed bits of blue and green, too. But when he heard that the cobras were real, the energy wavered immediately, pulled close to his body, and turned an ugly greenish-brown color."

"What was your experience, Amelia?" asked Äsha.

"I still can't see any colors, but I could feel what Matthew was talking about."

"Good. One of your talents, Amelia, is empathy. You're able to physically feel other people's feelings as if they're your own. It's as if the same message were written twice, in both French and German. Each of you reads and interprets a different language, but you still come up with the same message. So the fact that you 'feel' and Matthew 'sees' makes no difference. You each just need to concentrate on being as sensitive as you can be in your own particular area. Other areas of perception will open in time."

Chapter VI

The Dance of Light

All at once they were standing in a beautiful city, right below the Eiffel Tower. At first Amelia thought it must be Paris, but then she noticed the Statue of Liberty standing in a harbor with the Rock of Gibraltar in the background. She smiled, shook her head and decided not to bother asking any questions.

They had obviously just missed a huge downpour. The pavement was damp. Little streams rushed down gutters as droplets of water continued to fall from trees and flowers. Grey cumulus clouds were tinged with gold as the setting sun created the most spectacular triple rainbow Amelia had ever seen. Everything seemed renewed. The scent of spring combined with the wonderful fragrance of fresh bread and the smell of sauteed onions and garlic from a nearby restaurant.

"I'm starving!" exclaimed Amelia.

"Oh, me too!" added Matthew.

"Well, you're both on your own for a while," said Äsha. "There are lots of splendid restaurants and hotels. Go anywhere you like. Don't worry, you won't need money."

With that, Äsha disappeared.

Amelia and Matthew stared at each other, speechless. Then they both burst out laughing.

"Come on," said Matthew, "let's not even try to figure it out! How 'bout if we find a place to stay and then we'll get a bite to eat?"

"Where should we go?" said Amelia.

"Let's check out that hotel over there."

"You mean the one with the flowers? The place we'd never be able to afford?"

"Yep. That's the one."

Amelia laughed and said, "Okay!"

They walked along a cobblestone path bordering a beautiful park. They heard crickets and peeper frogs along with the sound of a waterfall hidden from view. The sweet fragrance of honeysuckle and jasmine clung heavily in the dense moisture. Deep, rich colors were interlaced with long, shadowy patterns caused by the setting sun. A couple of musicians played a harp and hammered dulcimer. The effect was magical.

Matthew reached out and held Amelia's hand. She looked at him and smiled despite the fact that her heart had skipped a beat or two.

He said, "You know, Amelia, this has been quite a memorable first date."

She laughed, "Just think, it isn't even over yet!"

He smiled and squeezed her hand.

Across the street from the park was the hotel. It was an elegant ten-story building and every floor had balconies with flower boxes. The walkway leading up to the hotel was composed of polished amethyst, rose and clear quartz. In the center was a beautiful green marble fountain with sculptures of dolphins leaping and playing in the water. At the top of the fountain was an incredible golden angel standing on a pink marble pedestal with water pouring out from where she stood.

The angel had long, wavy hair and the most beautiful face Amelia had ever seen. She wore a dress with a tight bodice. Draped softly across her breasts from the waist down the dress was full. With bare feet, the angel was standing, like a ballerina, up on the ball of her right foot with her left foot pointed and extended out behind her. Her arms were outstretched, palms down, and from her hands, jewels were suspended in midair: emeralds, rubies, sapphires, diamonds, different shades of topaz, pearls and amethyst. All of the jewels were huge, with perfect clarity. Engraved at the base of the fountain were the words:

THE DANCE OF LIGHT
To the Night
Have come the Dancers
Stars from the Heavens
Light on Earth
Seekers of the Searchers
Gently leading them Home

Amelia and Matthew stood and stared. Finally, Matthew said, "Can you see the colors around this fountain?"

"No, but I can certainly feel it," said Amelia. "What are you seeing?"

"Neon rainbow colors flecked with bits of gold," he said. "The colors have shapes and patterns that keep shifting and changing. It's like the colors are alive!"

"I know exactly what you mean!" exclaimed Amelia. "I can feel all of that. Look. The hair on my arms is standing on end."

"How strange," he said. "I'm not hungry or tired anymore."

He stepped back a couple paces and smiled. Amelia looked behind her, then back at Matthew.

"What?" she asked, a bit suspiciously.

"Amelia, you should see yourself. There's this pink and gold 'glow' around you. You're prettier than that angel."

Amelia instantly felt warmth and chills at the same time. Her cheeks were flushed. She had no idea what to say, so she smiled and simply said, "Thank you."

She stared at Matthew for a moment, wanting to share with him. She closed her eyes and without touching him, just let herself feel.

"You feel like sunshine," she said quietly, "and soft rain."

The Dance of Light

Amelia was a little surprised at herself for saying something that felt so intimate, but when she opened her eyes and saw the look on Matthew's face she knew he'd been genuinely touched. Matthew took Amelia's hands, looked deeply into her eyes and kissed her gently on the lips.

Amelia had read about first kisses, 'hearts leaping,' feeling ecstatic, but when she closed her eyes as Matthew kissed her, she saw colors. Soft pink, amethyst, opalescent white, the colors shifted and danced and seemed to have an energy all their own. She was simply an observer of the most beautiful light-show she'd ever seen.

After kissing Amelia, Matthew took a step back. Still holding her hands, he said, "Let me take a look at you." He led her over to a bench and they sat facing each other. He said, "I know this may sound strange, but remember what happened when you first looked into Äsha's eyes?"

Amelia nodded.

Matthew continued, "I get this feeling that if we just look at each other, without looking away, we'll both see something we haven't seen before."

She was quiet for a moment. With the exception of Äsha, Amelia had never looked at another person in this way before. As she looked at Matthew, he seemed so familiar. Looking at him was like running into an old acquaintance where they recognized each other but neither one could remember why.

Their eyes kept shifting back and forth not quite knowing where to focus. Amelia remembered something about the left side of the body being receptive, so she looked with her left eye into Matthew's left eye, and he held this gaze with her. At first her mind was racing. She'd read books, seen movies and been exposed to many lectures by her parents on safe sex and waiting until she was emotionally ready for sex, but nothing had prepared her for the depth of intimacy of simply looking into another person's eyes.

Amelia realized that once again she was barely breathing, so she took a few deep breaths and immediately felt more relaxed. She noticed a little smile in Matthew's eyes. After a minute or two, she realized he was breathing with her and as this happened she began to notice a strange pressure, a feeling of vibration, in her forehead. It wasn't painful like a headache, but it was a very definite sensation that she'd never felt before.

As Amelia continued to look into Matthew's eyes she suddenly felt herself "moving" down inside her own body. It was that feeling of being two places at once again. In the center of her "body" was a huge, beautiful, ancient tree with deep green leaves. She moved inside the tree and down into the roots and deep into the earth. It was dark and muddy and filled with swamp creatures and insects. She waded through the muck, climbed up onto solid land and there in front of her was Matthew. He hugged her and then walked with her over to a place with an invisible barrier.

At the barrier she was told that she had to give something to the gatekeeper in order to pass. Amelia had nothing, so she reached into her chest, pulled out her own heart, and handed it to the gatekeeper. Somehow she knew she was meant to go alone. As she walked she noticed there was a hole where her heart had been. She then saw a dry, hand-carved stone fountain. She climbed into the fountain and the fountain suddenly came to life, but instead of water, the fountain was moving, rainbow-colored light. She looked down and noticed that the light had filled the empty hole where her heart had been.

Amelia felt totally alive and filled with love. She stepped down from the fountain and saw Matthew on a huge, white horse with a long mane and tail. He was dressed as an armored knight. She noticed she was wearing a full, floor-length, sky-blue velvet dress that was tight through the bodice with a square neckline and long puffy sleeves tight from the elbow to the wrist. The dress was embroidered with real pearls around the neckline and on the sleeves.

Instantly she found herself sitting sideways in front of Matthew as he rode the horse. He had the reins in one hand and his other arm supported Amelia. They rode quietly through the forest for a while and then she found herself slipping off the horse. She thought she was going to fall but instead she felt herself supported by something invisible. She was gently placed on the ground. She then sat up in a kneeling position, sitting back on her heels.

Matthew climbed down from the horse. He stood above her; the armor flew off his body and disappeared instantly. He knelt directly in front of Amelia, took her hands, drew her up to him and embraced her.

She could see and feel a golden energy vortex swirling around them and then this golden light shot up into the sky. Immediately she felt herself being pulled up in the gold light and saw the base of a starship. The bottom was a bit like an angel food cake pan and she was traveling from the base right up through the center. She'd never seen anything like it before. Amelia's body jerked and she blinked for the first time.

Matthew smiled and said, "Where were you?"

"I was inside of myself . . . with you," said Amelia, feeling a bit confused.

"How odd," he said. "You and I were literally dancing in my heart; I mean my physical heart. And you were wearing this beautiful, blue velvet dress."

"Really?" she said.

"I reached into my pocket and I handed you this huge, perfect pearl. And suddenly we were standing inside a starship. We were surrounded by hundreds of people, and Amelia, we knew them all. You and I were walking side by side. It was some kind of a procession and the people stepped back, sort of creating an aisle for us as we walked. You were wearing a white dress instead of the blue one. It was kind of shimmery, and then I realized there was light woven into the dress. And you had flowers in your hair. We kept walking until we came to some people wearing white robes. Then you and I looked at each other the way we were looking at each other just now. And, not out loud but in our minds, we promised to *remember* each other." He paused for a moment and then said, "Does that make sense?"

Amelia nodded and told him about her experience. She said, "Do you think we were maybe seeing ourselves in the past and the future, that somehow we've come here out of our own future? Or is this all just in our imaginations?"

Matthew sat quietly for moment. Then he said, "Let's think about this one. You've said that you experienced past, present and future as happening all at once. Right?"

"Right."

"And Äsha says that everything takes place in consciousness. So if we were actually seeing our own past and future, it would have to take place in our minds."

"And that would feel like the imagination!" Amelia said excitedly. "If that's true, I wonder how many things we think we've made up when in fact we were actually seeing our own past or future, or maybe into another dimension."

"The way the yogi and the animals could see us in India," Matthew added.

"Well, just think. In the word 'imagination' is the word 'image,'" she said. "We just assume that because we see mental images we made it up because we think we're not connected to any other intelligence."

"So do you think this 'Source' that Äsha talks about, this Universal Intelligence, is something we have access to?" said Matthew.

Amelia thought for a moment. For some reason she saw the image of "time" in "layers" that were actually all one. Suddenly she had the feeling that the same was true of consciousness.

"I just had the strangest idea," she said. "Okay, we know we have a subconscious and a conscious mind. So what if we thought of the subconscious as being underground and the conscious mind as above ground. Wouldn't it make sense that we might have a 'higher' consciousness, like the air?

"Think about it, Matthew. What's the one thing we can't live without? We can live without water and food but not without air. We don't see it, we don't think about it, but it's always there. Wouldn't it make sense that there would be a consciousness surrounding us as close as the air we breathe that we might not be aware of any more than we'd be aware of standing on a gold mine unless we started digging?

"I've heard of people who instantly 'know' when someone has suddenly died in the family or there's been an accident," said Matthew. "If it's true there's a higher consciousness that knows everything, past, present and future, then I'll bet we're all somehow connected to everyone through that consciousness."

Suddenly, in her mind Amelia saw the image of a television.

"Of course!" she said. "It's like television. There's all kinds of information in the air around us but we don't even think about it unless we turn the T.V. on."

"Amelia, think of this. If a person didn't know that radio waves existed and you told him that there was music and talking and pictures in the air, he'd either think you were crazy or you had a lively imagination, right? So, if most people don't see or hear something they're going to say it's your imagination. Just because they haven't had the experience; not because it isn't true."

Amelia looked at Matthew and smiled, "We're getting pretty good at this. Äsha would be proud!" She leaned forward and said, "Are you getting hungry yet?"

"Famished!"

"Shall we get a bite to eat?"

"Sure. Let's just eat here at the hotel."

"Here!" said Amelia, "We could never afford to eat here."

"Amelia, we have no money, so what's the difference?"

"I thought if we went someplace cheaper we could just wash dishes for a day or two, instead of the rest of our lives!" she said.

"Come on, silly," said Matthew.

Holding hands, they walked into the hotel. The exterior elegance didn't even prepare them for the exquisite beauty inside. The ceilings were three stories high, covered with beautiful frescos painted with vivid colors and real gold. The floors were white marble except for an area in the center of the lobby where tall trees with song birds in their branches sprung from mossy ground with delicate wild flowers.

To their right was a spectacular stained-glass window. Not only was it 30 feet across and reached the ceiling, it was three-dimensional. There were three panels of glass, one behind the other, creating a feeling of depth. Though the sun had set, it appeared to be lit with real sunlight.

In the background were snow-capped mountains. In the middle were green hills and multicolored autumn trees. In the foreground were grapevines with big chunks of deep purple amethyst for grapes. The grapevines surrounded a real waterfall that seemed to emerge right out of the stained glass.

Amelia and Matthew walked up to the windows and just stared. Amelia looked at Matthew and said, "Can you feel these windows? There are chills running up and down my entire body."

"No kidding!" said Matthew. "I think I'm about to go into sensory overload!"

A bellman approached them, smiled and said, "Beautiful, aren't they?"

Matthew turned to him and said, "I've never seen colors like this before."

The bellman said, "That's because it isn't glass. What you see has been created from crushed diamonds, rubies, sapphires, emeralds, amethyst and a variety of topaz and some other precious stones." He paused for a moment and then said, "Would you like me to get your bags and arrange a room for you?"

Matthew said, "We don't have any bags and we don't have any money."

"I understand," said the bellman. "Would you still care for a room?"

"Well, actually, two adjoining rooms would be nice," said Matthew.

"I'll be right back," said the bellman.

During this conversation Amelia had been walking back and forth in front of the window. When the bellman left she walked over to Matthew and tugged on his sleeve.

"Get this!" she whispered, leading him to the other end of the window. "Look at the different colors on the floor," she said, turning Matthew away from the window. "Guess what I discovered? Now, close your eyes and don't look." She moved him to a yellow patch. His whole body was bathed in yellow.

"What?" he said.

"How do you feel?"

"Good. Like sunshine!"

"Okay, keep your eyes closed." Amelia then moved him to a purple patch. "Now how do you feel?"

Matthew stood there for a moment and said, "I feel the way I do after climbing all day and I'm finally standing on a mountain peak."

Once again Amelia took his arm and pulled him to a patch of green. Matthew peeked at her out of one eye. She didn't say a word, she just looked at him and raised her eyebrows in question. He said, "Peaceful. Tranquil. Sitting in a mountain meadow by a brook."

"Do you get it?" she said.

"What?"

"The colors! The colors! Each color makes you feel different."

"Oh! You're right!" he said. "Ha! I didn't even make that connection." Matthew walked into a blue patch and said, "Clean air, fresh breezes. My mind feels clear and strong. He stepped into pink. He looked at Amelia and smiled. "This is love," he laughed. "You always see pink hearts for Valentine's Day but I never thought you could *feel* pink. How funny!"

At that moment the bellman came back with their room key. "Shall I take you to your room?" he said.

"You can just give us the key," said Matthew.

"Very good," said the man. "Top floor."

"Thanks very much," said Matthew. He turned to Amelia and said, "Shall we check out the room first and then go eat?"

"Okay."

They took the elevator to the top floor and got off. There was only one door.

Amelia said, "Wait a minute! This is the penthouse!"

Matthew looked at the key and said, "It says 'P.H.' on the key. Well, it's worth a try!"

The Dance of Light

He put the key in the lock and the door opened. Slowly they stepped inside onto cherrywood floors with Persian rugs designed with pastel flowers. "Oh my!" gasped Amelia. The room had two-story ceilings and was filled with beautiful trees and plants. Delicate, fresh-cut flowers filled Oriental and crystal vases. Museum-worthy art work adorned the walls and next to a stained glass window was a grand piano.

The penthouse was in a circular shape with no exterior walls, only windows surrounded by an outdoor balcony. In the center of the penthouse was an arboretum filled with trees, wild flowers and birds, and a waterfall flowing into a series of pools with bright orange and white fish from Japan. The glass windows at the top were open to let in fresh air.

There were five bedrooms to choose from and Amelia knew immediately the room she wanted. It had a huge, antique bed. The headboard and footboard had delicate relief carvings in mahogany with scenes of horses and foals in a spring meadow. On the headboard the horses were grazing while the babies nursed or napped in the sunshine; at the foot of the bed the mares were running as the foals kicked up their heels. There was a down comforter and down pillows with white, cut-lace duvet and pillow covers. Pink, long-stemmed roses were next to the bed.

"I found my room!" said Amelia happily.

Matthew peeked in the doorway. "I'd say so!" he said. "I'll keep looking for mine."

Amelia opened the closet and inside was an entire wardrobe in her size, including shoes. There was an elegant box with real jewel necklaces, earrings and bracelets.

Amelia heard the doorbell ring and hurried to open the door. There stood a young woman barely older than Amelia with rosy cheeks, a round face, short cropped hair, and wearing a maid's uniform. She wasn't pretty in the classical sense but she had a great smile and a mischievous look in her eyes. Amelia felt sure she must have a good sense of humor.

"Hello! I'm Marie. I've come to help you get ready."

"Ready for what?" said Amelia.

"For dinner, of course!" said Marie.

"I didn't send for you."

"Of course not! May I come in?"

Amelia was puzzled but she opened the door. Instantly, Marie took Amelia's hand as if she were a playmate and, walking briskly to Amelia's room, she said, "Come. We'll have such fun!"

They walked through Amelia's room and Marie opened the bathroom door. Everything was white marble; the floors, the huge tub, the shower, even the sinks and the counters. The walls were mirrored and the room was lit with candlelight. A bubble bath had been drawn and smelled incredible. There were more plants and fresh-cut flowers.

"I'll get some other things ready while you bathe," said Marie. "There's a robe on the back of the door."

The Dance of Light

Marie left, closing the door behind her. Amelia peeled off her filthy, dirty hiking clothes and boots. She felt guilty putting them on the pristine, white floor but as she slipped into the warm bath all her cares and worries disappeared. She leaned back, looked up, and saw there was no ceiling. All she could see were stars glittering in the night. She felt every muscle in her body relax as she gave in to the soft, sensual aroma emanating from the bath.

It felt good to finally be alone for a few minutes. She ducked under the water and then shampooed her hair. Everything she needed was right beside the tub. Hunger was the only motivating force encouraging Amelia out of the tub. Otherwise, she would happily have drifted off to sleep. She got out, dried off, and then wrapped herself in a robe.

Marie knocked at the door. "Shall I help you get ready now?"

"Come in," said Amelia.

"Would you like me to dry your hair?"

"Thank you. That would be wonderful."

Marie used a device Amelia had never seen before and almost instantly her hair was dry. She then pulled Amelia's hair back with pearl combs. "Would you like me to help you with make-up?"

"I've never worn much make-up, but if you don't mind, that would be nice."

As Marie put make-up on Amelia she said, "You have such beautiful eyes, Amelia." Amelia looked at

Marie and saw that her eyes had the same intense blue of Äsha's eyes.

Amelia said, "You have eyes just like my friend."

"You mean Äsha?"

"You know Äsha?"

"Of course. We all know each other," replied Marie.

"Who's 'we'?"

"Well, actually we have many names here. We are called the Family of Light; Star Children; Light Workers; Children of Light. But we like to think of ourselves as Cosmic Renegades!"

Amelia paused and then said, "Who's in this 'Family'?"

"You and Matthew are Family members."

Amelia looked at her skeptically. Marie continued, "Don't you remember the people you saw when you were sitting outside?"

"No."

"Well, actually Matthew saw them, the ones on the starship."

"You know about those people?"

"But of course," said Marie. "I was there."

"Was that from our future?"

"I guess from your point of view it could be considered a future event that happened in your past."

The Dance of Light

"Never mind," said Amelia, shaking her head. "I shouldn't have asked."

"It's like drinking water from a stream. If you cup your hands you can hold the water, but if you try to grasp the water it will be gone. So don't grasp . . . just hold the idea. It will sink in."

"So what is the Family of Light?" asked Amelia.

"Didn't you read the inscription on the fountain outside?"

"I did, but I don't know what it meant."

Marie recited the poem. "'To the Night have come the Dancers. Stars from the Heavens, Light on Earth, Seekers of the Searchers, Gently leading them Home.' Now, think creatively, Amelia, not analytically. The poem says, 'To the Night . . . .' What does night mean to you?"

"Darkness?"

"What is darkness? I mean that in the most simple sense. If you're in a dark room, what causes the darkness?"

"Oh. Well, having no light."

"Right. So, what's light? Keep it simple."

"Well, let's see. Physically, it's heat, power, energy. It has different wavelengths and vibrations and colors."

"Good," said Marie. "What's another definition of light? You know, like a little 'light' on the subject, or 'lighten up,' or a person who's 'light'?"

"Okay. It would mean knowledge, understanding, humor. And a person who's 'light' would be happy, not too serious."

"So, from that point of view, what does 'darkness' mean?"

"Ignorance?"

"Yes. What else? What's behind ignorance?"

Amelia thought for a moment and said, "Well I guess people who are ignorant are afraid of something they don't understand."

"Yes . . . ?"

"Oh, of course. Fear."

"There you go. Fear is the bottom line of *any* negative emotion."

"Fear of what?"

"Fear of the future, based on the past, is on the surface. But the deepest fear that everyone on the planet faces is the fear that they're not worth loving."

Amelia said, "Sometimes I get angry with my mother because I think she doesn't understand me. I know she loves me but sometimes she doesn't think about how I feel."

"Even though you know your mother loves you," said Marie, "don't you feel that if she loved you a little more then she'd understand you? She'd love you enough to think about how you feel?"

"I guess that's true."

The Dance of Light

"Isn't fear always about 'not enough' in the past or the future?" asked Marie. "Now, where were we? Oh, yes. We've managed to get through the first line of the poem. Let's add the second line. 'To the Night have come the Dancers.' What do you think is the meaning of 'the Dancers'?"

"I don't know."

"What do you feel when you're dancing?"

"I love to dance! I feel happy, energetic, sort of carried away by the music."

"Do you try to hurry to the end of the song?"

"No. That would be missing the whole point."

"And what 'point' is that?"

"Well, dancing is creative and spontaneous. You can't hurry. That would take all the fun out of it."

"In other words," said Marie, "when you dance, you're present -- in the moment, so to speak."

"Exactly."

"So the 'Dancers' would be those who know how to be present and full of joy and energy. Resembling *light*, wouldn't you say?"

"I see."

"Thus far, then, the poem means that the 'Dancers' are those who live in a *present* consciousness of *light*, joy, passion, love, grace, movement, freedom. They're spirited and energetic. And they've chosen to bring this light -- in other words, their own understanding -- into the Night;

the darkness of ignorance, fear, lack, limitation, the belief that there's not enough love. Is this all clear, Amelia?"

"Got it!"

"The next line says, 'Stars from the Heavens, Light on Earth,'" said Marie as she began curling Amelia's hair.

Amelia thought for a moment. She flashed on some of her earlier experiences. She thought of herself "dancing among the stars" and remembered Äsha saying she was "home." Then she thought of the "light-beings" and felt what it was like when she was "light" and when she realized that Äsha was light.

She looked at Marie. "Are you light . . . when you're not in that body?"

Marie just smiled.

"You are, aren't you?" said Amelia.

Marie held Amelia's gaze and said, "Aren't you?"

Amelia thought about that for a moment and said, "When I was with Äsha, I felt myself floating among stars and Äsha said that I'd been 'home'. Am I, are we, from another star system?"

"Ah, now there's something to think about," said Marie.

Amelia's mind was galloping. "How's that possible?"

"You mean, how could you look and grow up like an earthling and not be from Earth?"

"Yes. I don't understand."

The Dance of Light

"If you were going into outer space wouldn't you wear a space suit to protect you from the environment?" said Marie.

"Of course."

"People are very frightened on earth. You know it is quite an insane place to live."

Amelia nodded.

"In this primitive place, if we showed up as beams of light we would surely be killed or dissected, don't you think? Let me put it this way: You had to be 'born' into your Earth space suit partially to protect you from the environment but mostly to protect you from the fear and ignorance of the inhabitants. And you don't take it off until you quit, or you've done what you came here to do. You know, 'When in Rome look like the Romans.'"

"Actually, the phrase is 'When in Rome *do* as the Romans.'"

"That too! You learn how to *do* as the Romans. That's why most everyone here is a human-*doing* instead of a human-*being*. You grow up doing lunch as easily as you do dysfunction. Then you get to blend with the rest of the planet, except some people don't get to do the lunch part. Then, once you've really learned to blend and look like a native, that's when your DNA goes off like a timer."

"Now you've lost me! Completely!"

Children of Light

"Do you remember Shakespeare saying something like, 'All the world's a stage and there are many players playing different parts'?" asked Marie.

"I vaguely remember that."

"So it's like you're a 'player.' Only in this case you're already a star. That's kind of a joke. It's okay to laugh, Amelia."

"I'm sorry. I think I'm trying too hard."

"There you have it! Now where were we? Oh, yes. So, you're a player on the Earth-stage. But that's not who you really are."

"So, who am I really?" said Amelia.

"In a nutshell? You're a star child. Now, look. This is a long story. It would be much easier for you to whiz into another dimension, which in your terms would be going back through time."

Amelia said, "How do I do tha . . . ?"

Chapter VII

Star Children

Before the question was fully out of her mouth she found herself floating above the newly-formed earth. She was able to look at any place and "zoom in" to the smallest detail or pull back and get an overview. It wasn't at all the way she thought it would be. The earth was a fantasy land. There weren't just people, there were elves and fairies, marvelous shape-shifters and all kinds of spectacular creatures. Everyone knew how to "manifest" whatever they wanted or needed, right out of thin air. And there was no sense of "higher" or "lower" intelligence. Even stones and crystals were known as record keepers and were held in high regard for their ability to contain light. All life forms respected each other and they had perfect freedom to think and act as they pleased.

Amelia realized the light she was seeing wasn't just from the sun. She could see there were "beings" from other dimensions that were drawn to the planet. In the same way that Amelia had seen light around herself earlier, she saw a light "energy" around the planet. And these "beings" were sort of basking in the light. They were quite benevolent and Amelia had the feeling that some of them were actually responsible for the creation of the planet.

Children of Light

In the same way that one could feel really happy and energized after seeing a good movie or feel the pleasure of soaking in the sunshine these beings enjoyed the energy from the earth and in turn radiated "light-energy" themselves.

But there were also beings who didn't like the light. Amelia had no judgments against these "dark-ones" because, for some reason, she was able to feel their feelings as if they were her own.

"What do they feel like?" Surprised, Amelia turned to see Marie next to her.

"Marie! I'm so glad you're here." Then she thought about Marie's question. "What do they feel like?" repeated Amelia. "Well, I don't know if this is the actual story, but I can tell you how they feel to me on an emotional level. It feels as if their civilization has lived underground for generations, frightened of what might be on the surface. And they're so afraid of themselves that they've shut down all their emotions. They feel nothing."

Amelia paused for a moment, trying to frame the answer perfectly. She said, "Then they come up out of their caverns into the bright sunshine and it's unbearably painful. They want to live above ground but they hate the light. They've been afraid for so long that joy seems frivolous and freedom is frightening . . . like a bee leaving its colony to live alone. To the bee, it's death."

Marie nodded and said, "You're very good, you know. And you're quite right. To us, their life underground would be imprisonment; to them, it's safe and secure. Now watch what happens."

Time moved swiftly and Amelia saw the dark-ones try to take over the planet on this higher-dimensional level from the light-beings. There was a war and in the end the light-beings lost. The dark-ones brought darkness to Earth in the form of ignorance and fear. They placed an energetic force-field around the planet so that light and knowledge couldn't reach the inhabitants. The beings on the earth were hypnotized into "forgetting" who they were and what life had been like before the dark-ones took over the planet. There were some stories but they were called fairy tales and myths and people who believed them were criticized and quickly felt stupid.

Amelia turned to Marie and said, "I don't get it. Why did they have to fight?"

"You must begin to understand it 'energetically,'" said Marie. "The dark-ones live off of dark-energy: fear, anger, resentment. The light-beings feed on light-energy: love, joy, enthusiasm, understanding. Think about it. You couldn't grow rice and wheat in the same field at the same time. If you flood the field for the rice, the wheat dies. If you keep it drier for the wheat, the rice dies. So, from a logical point of view, the dark-ones wanted their crop in the field."

"But how do they live on other people's energy?" asked Amelia.

"Remember, you're dealing with other dimensions. What you eat is or was alive. It had energy . . . Life-force. On higher dimensions they skip the physical part because they aren't in physical form and they live directly off of energy."

"Well, why would they come to us here on Earth? For energy?"

"Because people on Earth have *emotions!*" said Marie.

"So?"

"Think, Amelia! Have you ever walked into a room after two people have had a huge argument? What does it feel like?"

"Thick. It's like walking into a brick wall."

"And what emotions are present?"

"Anger, resentment, maybe betrayal."

"And of course the list can go on and on. So, keeping in mind the energy that two people can generate, now think of the possibilities when you multiply it by an entire planet that's fearful and angry. Get the picture?"

"You're saying that the more fear and anger there are on the planet, the more the dark-ones are well-fed?"

"That's it!" said Marie.

"So, why are we here?"

"Basically, we're here to cut off their food supply. If the inhabitants here can shift from living in fear to a place of light and understanding, that's where we come in as the 'Dancers.' Remember? Then the dark-ones would either have to switch to light-energy food or go find another dysfunctional planet."

"That's it?"

"I know it's remarkably simple, but it can be a bit of a challenge bringing the potential 'dancers' of the world 'out of the closet'! Let's look at it like a play. And let's say that for a few hundred thousand years the dark-ones have been the audience and, though the plot changes daily, the play always remains a tragedy. Now, there are a couple of rules. The dark-ones have to stay in the audience, they can't just jump up on the stage and change the plot or become the director. And the second rule is that the actors, just before going on-stage, agree to forget who they really are and where they came from. They're just acting a part but they get to be totally spontaneous, creating the drama as they go along." Marie stopped, looked at Amelia, and said, "Are you with me so far?"

"I think so."

"So let's suppose you've had the same old actors, wearing different costumes, creating the same basic drama year after year after year. A boring variation on a theme of malice, mayhem and murder, but the audience still likes it. Then one day some of the actors get together and decide they're tired of high drama and tragedy, but there are too few of them so their attempts to 'lighten up' the show end up being nothing more than cameo, bit parts, like the court jester in 'Hamlet.'"

"I thought the court jester was just a 'skull' in Hamlet," said Amelia.

"Very good," said Marie, smiling. "You're quick!"

Amelia wasn't sure if Marie really knew that tidbit of information or if she were just good with a quick comeback, but she laughed all the same.

"So, now the plot thickens!" said Marie. "Let's say these few but determined actors send an all-points bulletin out into the cosmos. It reads something like: 'Looking for a few good stars to play actors. Tough Audience: No Drama-Queens or Axe-Murderers need apply.'"

Amelia laughed, "You should be in show business, Marie!"

"What do you think I'm doing here?" she replied.

They both laughed. "Now, where was I?" said Marie. "These moments of mirth and levity always throw me off. Ah, yes! Star children love a challenge. They travel the cosmos looking in the Universal Want Ads for words like: Impossible Situation; Never Before; and of course, our favorite, 'Tough Audience.'"

"What do you mean, 'tough audience'? What will they do? Boo, hiss and throw rotten tomatoes?" said Amelia.

"No," said Marie. "If the dark-ones don't like the play, remember, they can't interfere *physically*, but as long as they stay in their seats they can hypnotize the actors into forgetting that they were going to act differently and change the plot from a tragedy to a comedy or a love story."

"So, where do the star children fit in?" asked Amelia.

"Like I said, they love a challenge," said Marie. "In your school system on Earth, they'll be the renegades, the misfits or the nerds; at best, considered extremely 'different' by their peers. But I digress. Back to the plot!"

Amelia shook her head and wondered to herself whether or not she would ever make it back for dinner.

"Of course you'll make it back for dinner!" retorted Marie, "but first we have a few more fish to fry!"

"Can't I even have my own thoughts?" wailed Amelia.

"Sorry," said Marie. "Okay, I'll wrap it up quickly! Should we leave the heads on or off?"

Amelia shook her head again.

"Sorry, just kidding! You know tying in the fish with murder and mayhem, the court jester. Never mind, dumb joke!" Marie struck a noble pose and said, "To decapitate or not decapitate? That is the question."

"Marie! What's the point?" said Amelia, stamping her foot (which isn't easy when you're floating in midair).

"Right. I'm back! No more jokes," said Marie. "So, the star children join the troupe. They go along with all the rules and regulations and forget who they are before going on stage. But in the same way that the dark-ones sort of cheat by hypnotizing the actors, the star children pack an alarm clock inside their costume. Well actually the alarm is right in their body, but that's hard to explain unless you understand a lot about DNA." She looked at Amelia skeptically and said, "Do you?"

"Understand a lot about DNA? No," said Amelia.

"Okay, then, an alarm clock," said Marie.

"Right," said Amelia, nodding her head. "We need more teachers like you in school, Marie. Even if we never figure out what you're talking about, at least we'll be entertained!"

"There you have it!" said Marie. "From the mouths of babes!"

"What are you, a year older than I am?" said Amelia.

"To be quite honest," said Marie quietly, looking around to be sure no one was eavesdropping, "I've probably got at least a billion years on you." She winked, put her finger to her lips and said, "Shh, don't tell anyone."

Amelia nodded and said confidentially, "It'll be our little secret."

"What I was about to say," continued Marie, "was that if everyone were simply 'entertained' on stage (or in life, as the case may be) and saw the humor in everything, my job would be finished. I could tackle another dysfunctional planet instead. Quickly, back to the alarm clock concept! You see, the star children have gone through years of rigorous training before attempting to go on-stage. And just to be on the safe side, they pack this 'alarm clock' on stage under their costumes. They play along, become dysfunctional like everyone else, but they have their alarm set to go off in adulthood or when the planet is just about to self-destruct, whichever comes first."

"I would assume my alarm has gone off," said Amelia, "based on results. And since I'm not really an adult yet, does that mean the planet is about to self-destruct?"

"In a word," said Marie, "Yes. We won't discuss that now however. We're still trying to get you back in time for dinner. But since there's no time, that shouldn't be a problem."

"However, I am hungry 'in the moment,' as you like to say," Amelia replied.

"Oh, you poor dear," said Marie. "Would you like to go back now?"

"First, I want to hear the end of this story, and then I would dearly love to go back and eat. I do still have a body, as far as I know, or at least I still believe I'm capable of being hungry," said Amelia laughing.

"Well, the alarm has to be subtle. That way the audience doesn't know when it's going off," said Marie. "So the star children set their alarms on 'vibrate.' If it works, and it doesn't always, the star child gradually begins to wake up. The star children, because they remember who they are, have a lot of power on stage. But there's a problem."

"What's that?" said Amelia, now thoroughly interested.

"Well, you see," replied Marie, "when a star child wakes up, it's obvious pretty quickly. Mentally speaking, they look like marathon runners among couch-potatoes. Not too tricky to spot. So the dark-ones sit in the audience and have fun throwing mental, hypnotic pictures at the star children. It's not really a problem unless the negative mental picture is something the star child happens to believe about himself anyhow."

"If the star children are trained before they come here, why don't they know that they're just seeing an illusion?"

"They've been well trained in dysfunction, too! It's not always easy to forget everything you learned and only remember what you know. The problem is that some star children either refuse to wake up or when they do wake up and remember who they are and where they came from they get homesick and want to leave as soon as possible."

"How do they leave?" said Amelia.

"They simply 'do as the Romans.' Create a good drama," said Marie. It doesn't matter . . . a car accident, a good fatal disease. They usually know better than suicide, but a heart attack or cancer will do."

"But why death? Isn't there another way to go?" said Amelia.

"Well, there is the route of the Ascended Masters, people like Jesus, who just disappeared. But they're a little different from the ones who are scrambling to get back to their own star system. No, Amelia dear. When on stage you can't just float away like Mary Poppins or Peter Pan. The play's the thing! Drama is what counts and it's got to be believable!"

"So these particular star children wake up," said Amelia, "after spending years in training, and then even more time becoming fully dysfunctional, they know what they're here to do but then they decide they don't want to do it? Is that it?"

Marie nodded.

"In other words, they're weenies!" said Amelia, laughing.

"That concept might be a tad judgmental," said Marie, trying halfheartedly to cover her amusement, "but nonetheless, pretty accurate. However, in all fairness, everyone always has a choice. This is still a freewill zone."

"So what about all the star children who wake up and say, 'Let's Go!'" said Amelia.

"That's what you're doing right now. You're in the process of de-programming. How does it feel?" Marie asked brightly.

Amelia cocked her head, half smiled and said, "I could describe a whole range of emotions to answer that question! At least I'm not feeling like a smorgasbord for the dark-ones. I feel more like a sack lunch working my way toward being a Happy Meal!"

Marie laughed and said, "Once you're fully de-programmed and your true memory returns, that's when 'the game's afoot.' That's when you start looking like the marathon runner amongst couch potatoes and that's when the mental fun and games begin. At all costs, Amelia, maintain your *sense of humor!*"

They laughed and Amelia found herself back in the penthouse bathroom.

"Oh dear," said Marie. "I forgot to tell you the rest of the space suit story."

"You do have quite the memory," said Amelia.

"Well, when you do finally take off your Earth space suit," said Marie, "some people call it death. You get to be your very own light-self again. But I must tell you, Amelia, this thing called 'death' that everyone's so afraid of: It's because they've never experienced death. They've only observed it. It can be quite exhilarating and freeing to leave this dense body. You've already felt that freedom, haven't you?"

Astounded, Amelia asked, "You mean that's what death is like?"

"For some. Not for everyone," said Marie. "As with life on earth, death is also an interpretation. Some people are very attached to having a body. Imagine being a chain-smoker or an alcoholic and suddenly you don't have a body with which to smoke or drink."

Amelia was puzzled. "But if the person no longer had a body, why would they want to smoke or drink?" she said.

"Because the desire is mental, not physical. Remember, what a person *believes* is stronger than what actually is. If a person believes they're addicted, they will go on feeling and thinking like an addict even if there's no physical body. It's like 'cold-turkey'. There's no alcohol, no cigarettes. Yet there's still the same desire. Some addictions are in the form of attachments. Some people are so deeply attached to their families and loved ones that they simply won't let go."

"Well, isn't that because they love them?" said Amelia.

"No, it's different," said Marie. She finished Amelia's hair and then picked up a dress that was lying across a chair and held it up for Amelia to see. "What do you think?" she said.

"Oh, it's beautiful," said Amelia.

"Underwear's in the top drawer," said Marie, discreetly stepping out of the bathroom.

Amelia got dressed. Everything right down to her shoes and stockings fit perfectly. She wore a long, white silk slip under an antique, white lace dress with a low neckline. She turned to see herself in the mirror. She looked like a princess with her hair in curls held away from her face with pearl combs. The dress was a bit daring, but Amelia had never had enough of a figure before to be daring. She smiled as she saw how feminine and curvy she'd become. Marie reappeared, quietly buttoned up the back of her dress and then put a diamond and pearl choker around Amelia's neck.

"Do you like it?" she said, clasping the necklace.

"It's gorgeous!" said Amelia, happily. "I hope Matthew knows how we're dressing."

"Don't worry," said Marie, "he's being helped too. Now let me see you."

Amelia turned around and smiled. Marie opened a crystal bottle of perfume and held it for Amelia to smell.

"Yes?" Marie said.

"Definitely!" said Amelia.

"Oh, my. You're so beautiful and radiant. How could you not know that you're 'light'?" Marie said, smiling warmly. "Are you ready to go?"

"Yes, but what about the rest of the poem?" said Amelia, a bit urgently.

"Oh, well it'll be revealed to you, the meaning. Don't worry."

"Will you at least finish what you were telling me about people who are attached to their families and love?" said Amelia.

"Alright," said Marie, "we'll take just a moment. Remember when we talked about the 'Dancers'? Ones who are fully present, full of energy, living in joy? If you were dancing for an audience, you'd express the same joy you feel in the music and your love of dancing to everyone. Right?"

"Of course," said Amelia.

"You wouldn't dance beautifully for part of the audience and turn your back on the others. It's the same idea with love. When you're truly loving, it comes from inside, from who you're being, and radiates out to others. Not because of who they are, but because of who you are, who you're choosing to be."

"What does that have to do with people being attached and unable to let go?" said Amelia.

"When people cannot let go, it's because they don't see themselves as whole. Their identity is Mother; Father; Daughter; Wife; Son; Grandparent; Single; Divorced; Married. They've spent their lives living an identity they're very attached to. And since this identity is attached to family and friends, then without these people they think they're lost. A woman, for instance, may have a drama that says, 'Who am I if I'm not Billy's mother, or my mother's daughter?' Or, 'My husband needs me; he can't get along without me.' This type of perception stops people from moving on because they don't trust that everything has a purpose."

"So what should people do?" said Amelia.

"It sounds like a contradiction," said Marie, "but people need to learn to be lovingly detached."

"You're right. That does sound like a contradiction," said Amelia.

"Imagine living in such a way," said Marie, "that you're always loving and caring toward everyone equally, including yourself, without making some people special and others less important. So the idea of being loving, yet detached, is like the sun: it shines equally and impartially on everyone and everything. There's no judgment. It doesn't matter whether a person is a saint or a sinner. The sun just shines. Nature mirrors reality, Amelia."

"I know this is off the subject," said Amelia, "but what you just said about nature and reality reminded me of something. I know about conscious and subconscious, but is there a 'higher' consciousness?"

"Why of course!" said Marie. "How could we live without it?"

"That's what I thought," said Amelia, excited, "just like the air we breathe!"

"Only closer," said Marie.

There was a knock at the door. They walked across the bedroom and Marie opened the door for Amelia. Matthew was wearing a handmade Italian suit. His hair hung loosely around his shoulders and, for the first time, Amelia saw him without his glasses. She was genuinely surprised to see how beautiful his eyes were and how wonderful he looked dressed up.

Her surprise was nothing, however, compared to Matthew's amazement when he saw Amelia. He'd never seen her with make-up, or in a dress, or with her hair curled. Actually, Amelia had never done all those things at once before. It wasn't becoming of a good tomboy.

She'd felt a little embarrassed by how feminine she looked and she was feeling a bit out of place until she saw the stunned look on Matthew's face. She felt like Cinderella at the ball with Marie as her fairy godmother.

Matthew seemed unable to move and just stood staring at Amelia. Finally, Marie came to the rescue, stuck her hand out and said, "Hello, Matthew. I'm Marie." He went to shake her hand but suddenly stopped.

"Don't I know you?" he said.

She smiled, "Amelia will tell you why you know me. It's a long story."

Matthew looked puzzled. He shook Marie's hand and said, "Nice to meet you." Then he looked at Amelia, smiled and said, "Are you still hungry?"

"Are you kidding?" said Marie, interrupting. "That's all she's been talking about for the last hour!"

Amelia laughed, gave Marie a hug and said, "Thanks for everything."

"I'm always at your service."

Amelia and Matthew took the elevator down to the hotel restaurant and Amelia told him about Marie being on the starship he'd seen in his vision.

The maître d' greeted them and Matthew said, "I know this is an odd thing to say, but we have no money."

"Of course you don't," said the man. "Would you prefer to sit outdoors or in this evening?"

"Outdoors?" he said, looking at Amelia. She nodded.

They stepped outside into fairyland. Before them spread a full acre of trees laced with tiny white lights. They saw flowers of every color imaginable and the sweet smell of gardenia and jasmine permeated the garden. There were lit walkways and arched bridges over streams, waterfalls lit from behind, and ponds with white swans floating majestically. The evening was a perfect temperature, the sky was filled with stars, and a quartet played Mozart.

All the tables were quite private and situated inconspicuously throughout the garden. They were seated at a candle-lit table with a lace cloth and fresh roses under a beautiful old oak tree. They sat quietly for a few moments just looking at each other.

Finally, Amelia said, "I've never seen you without your glasses before. You have beautiful eyes."

Matthew looked a little embarrassed but smiled and said, "It's the strangest thing. I took my glasses off to take a shower and when I got out I realized I could see. I don't know why. Isn't that funny?"

He looked at Amelia quietly for a moment and said, "I don't think anyone has ever seen you the way I'm seeing you tonight. It's not just how you look. It's that I've seen you inside. We've danced in my heart!"

Suddenly he stopped. "You know what, I just thought of something. Would you like to dance with me?"

Amelia smiled and said, "Sure."

"But I want to try something different," he said. "I can't begin to tell you what it was like when you and I were dancing in my heart. I've been thinking about that all night. Now, you'll have to use your imagination for this, so just close your eyes for a second."

Amelia nodded and closed her eyes.

Matthew continued, "Imagine the two of us dancing inside your physical heart. Got it?"

Amelia smiled and nodded.

"Now, imagine us dancing in my heart at the same time," he said.

He watched Amelia with her eyes still closed. As she held this image her face lit up. Then she opened her eyes and smiled at him.

"The idea is," he said, "we'll do that while we're dancing with each other. So we'll be dancing inside-and-out!"

"Do you want to make it even a little more interesting?" said Amelia with a wry smile.

"Sure!" exclaimed Matthew.

"Let me tell you what I saw along with the other things you were telling me to do. You close your eyes this time. Imagine a space about the size of a small fist two inches out from the center of your chest."

Amelia touched Matthew's chest about eight inches below his collar bone and said, "Right out from here," Matthew nodded.

"I don't know why, but this place I'm describing has something to do with the heart and that energy we see outside of the body. Anyhow, in that space, imagine hundreds of thousands of stars whirling and dancing and you're right there in the center," she said.

She paused for a few moments and said, "Now just imagine becoming one of the stars. Golden-white light comes right out of you like you're the sun. And then see me the same way."

Matthew started to smile and Amelia smiled just watching him.

"So, as we're dancing in each other's hearts," she said, "we're also dancing among the stars as *light*!"

Matthew opened his eyes, smiled broadly, and said, "It's the 'E' ticket again, Amelia!"

"Do you think we can do all of that," said Amelia, "and still dance at the same time?"

"Absolutely!" he replied, standing up and offering her his hand.

They walked hand in hand through the garden to the elegant hardwood dance floor just as the quartet began playing a lovely waltz. The dance floor was empty.

Matthew looked at Amelia and said, "You don't happen to know how to waltz, do you?"

Amelia smiled. "I was raised on classical music. That's the only thing my parents would allow in our home. My father taught me to waltz when I was eight. What about you? Can you waltz?"

He smiled, "My mother met my father when she was teaching ballroom dance at Arthur Murray." He raised his eyebrows and said, "Need I say more?"

As they stepped onto the floor and began to dance, Amelia realized that she'd only danced with her father, which she always enjoyed, but dancing with Matthew brought a whole new meaning to the word.

They were the perfect height for each other and the dancing flowed effortlessly. Amelia could sense people staring at them. Then she remembered to imagine all the things they'd talked about. As she did this, she felt as if she were floating. It was the most incredible feeling dancing inside-and-out. The dances inside were all different.

In her own heart, she danced as a ballerina in bare feet, with her hair down, wearing a flowing, white silk dress. A light breeze softly blew her hair and dress. Matthew danced as a ballet partner would, holding her, supporting her as she turned, and effortlessly lifted her up into the air.

The image Amelia saw of them dancing in Matthew's heart was less structured. It was more like playing outdoors, splashing through streams, and dancing in a sunlit field, but with no gravity so they could leap and fly through the air!

Where Amelia felt the most connected to Matthew was in the space with the stars. She felt the feeling of love and understanding that she'd felt with the luminous man in the library. She realized these 'heart-spaces' with the stars were two inches away, which meant that when they danced with each other these spaces would be merged with one another, especially because they were so close to the same height with Amelia wearing high heels.

Amelia couldn't imagine that actually making love could be any better than this. "Well, maybe different," she thought, "but not better." Pictures, colors and feelings all danced through her body, rushing, swirling, pouring out. Then she thought of the poem. "To the Night have come the Dancers." She never realized the power of that idea until this very moment. *"This* is what the 'Dancers' are bringing!" she thought.

Suddenly the poem clicked. "Stars from the Heavens, Light on Earth" wasn't just about being from another star system. It was about *being* this light-energy she felt as she danced with Matthew; and that was the meaning of Light on Earth.

Amelia still wasn't quite sure about the next two lines, "Seekers of the Searchers, Gently leading them Home," but she felt good that she'd figured out two other lines all by herself.

The song ended and a slow song began. As they swayed slowly, Matthew and Amelia looked at each other the way they did by the fountain earlier that day. Matthew said, "Are you still dancing with me everywhere?"

Amelia smiled and nodded.

He smiled and squeezed her hand. "Good," he said quietly.

Then Amelia noticed that in her 'star-heart' Matthew was kissing her. She smiled and asked, "What are you doing in that space with the stars?"

"I'm kissing you. Did you know?"

Amelia nodded and said, "Matthew, inside it feels exactly the same as when you really did kiss me."

Matthew's eyes were glowing. "I know," he said. "Isn't it funny to think of what you can get away with in public?"

Amelia laughed, "You're so funny."

Matthew put his arm around Amelia's waist and they started walking back to their table. He said, "How many days do you think it's been since we've eaten?"

She laughed, "It's impossible to tell when you're time traveling."

"And dimension-hopping!" he added.

They sat down at their table and the waiter appeared with their meals. They were each served their favorite meal with their favorite drinks.

Surprised, Amelia looked at Matthew after the waiter left and said, "Did you order for me?"

"No," he said, looking equally surprised.

"That reminds me," said Amelia. "Did your room have an entire wardrobe in your size?"

"It did!" he said. "Yours too?"

She nodded. "Was there someone to help you get ready, too?"

"Oh yeah," he said. "I forgot to tell you about that."

They discussed what they learned while getting ready and, though their experiences were a little different, they both had a fairly good grasp of all the same ideas.

They finished their meals and then strolled through the garden with their arms around each other. Finally, exhaustion pulled them back to the penthouse suite. They stepped inside. Candles and oil lamps had been lit throughout and their beds were turned back.

Matthew walked with Amelia to her room. He hugged her and kissed her on the forehead. "Tonight you'll be sleeping right here," he said sweetly, putting his hand over his heart. "Goodnight," he said smiling.

Amelia smiled, put her hands on his cheeks, looked directly into his eyes and without ever shifting her gaze, kissed him lightly on the lips.

"Goodnight," she said.

She floated into her room and thought, "The days of chivalry are not dead." She found a beautiful, embroidered silk nightgown laid across the foot of the bed. She undressed quickly, put on the nightgown, and was sound asleep the moment her head hit the pillow.

Chapter VIII

99.9999% Empty Space

Amelia awoke to bright sunshine streaming through her windows. She could hear birds singing in the arboretum and the soothing sound of the waterfall. There was a soft knock on her door.

"Come in," she said, sitting up in bed, pulling her knees up in front of her.

"Good morning, sleepyhead," said Matthew, carrying a silver tray and setting it by her bed.

Amelia thought he looked quite handsome wearing forest green corduroys with a brown leather belt and a white shirt open at the collar.

"What have we here?" asked Amelia

Matthew lifted the silver lid and said, "Viola!"

Amelia laughed, "Isn't it *voilà*?"

"No," said Matthew, smiling. "It's breakfast!"

There was fresh juice in crystal goblets, all kinds of exotic fresh fruits - some Amelia had never seen before - along with raspberries, strawberries and blueberries. There were also freshly baked croissants with butter and a selection of homemade fruit preserves.

"This looks incredible!" said Amelia.

"It's called a continental breakfast," said Matthew. "We're on the continent you know."

"The question is: The 'continent' in what dimension?"

"Now there's something to ponder over breakfast!"

"Would you like to join me?" said Amelia, patting the bed next to her.

"Ah, but of course, Chèrie!" said Matthew in his best French accent.

He picked up the tray, went around to the other side of the bed and set the tray in the middle. They ate breakfast and decided to spend the morning walking in the park and taking in a few sights. Matthew left with the tray. Amelia hopped out of bed and looked through the closet. She found some linen pants with a matching jacket and a coral colored silk blouse.

In the mirror it looked as if everything had been tailored to fit her. Her hair was still curly from the night before and she found a great hat that matched the outfit perfectly. There was matching lipstick in the bathroom vanity and she added a little makeup to the remainder from the night before. She smiled at herself in the mirror and had to admit she liked herself this way.

Amelia and Matthew walked over to the park across the street from the hotel and wandered over to watch a painter. He was wearing a red beret and an artist's smock. He had dark, ringlet curls, rosy cheeks and green eyes. He appeared to be right out of a painting himself.

He turned and said, "Howdy! Lovely morning isn't it? Would mademoiselle care to have her portrait painted?"

"Oh, thank you," said Amelia, "but we have no money."

"Money. Now that's a word I haven't heard in a long time!" he said. "You're not from here, are you?"

"No."

"Well, we have no need of money here."

"Why not?" said Amelia. "How do you buy things?"

"It's kind of a long story," he said. "How about if I paint your portrait while I explain?"

"Alright. Thank you," said Amelia, sitting down on the chair he offered her.

"To begin with, my name is Timothy and today I am an artist. A very happy artist, I might add, having such a lovely subject to work with!"

Before Amelia or Matthew could introduce themselves Timothy continued as if there was no need for an introduction.

"There is no need for money because here we recognize that things are thoughts. You're both familiar with this concept aren't you?" Timothy said.

"We're working on it," said Matthew.

"Whatever you can imagine, you can create through the power of your own intention," said Timothy, dabbing a bit of color on the portrait. "If you want a castle on the hillside with a Rolls Royce and stable full of horses, you can have it. You can mingle with the jet-set crowd and go to all the best parties, see the world, or the universe if you prefer."

"What if two people wanted the same castle? They couldn't both live in the same place," said Amelia.

"Why not?" replied Timothy. "Couldn't you and Matthew both dream that you lived in King Arthur's castle and not be sharing the same dream? You could be in the same 'place' and still be in your own 'world,' so to speak."

"I think you've lost me," said Matthew.

"Let's take something you know is a concept," said Timothy. "Suppose you believed mathematics was a thing and not a thought. Numbers would have to be in a material form. Let's say the numbers are made out of wood or metal and you had to buy a certain amount of numbers in order to balance your checkbook or pay your bills. Now, imagine there's a time when numbers were in high demand, like at tax time. And suppose they started running out of sevens and fives. All of a sudden people would be scrambling to buy and trade those numbers. Stock market prices would skyrocket far beyond what they were really worth. But that could only happen if you didn't understand that numbers are concepts. Do you see?"

Amelia and Matthew nodded.

"So, it's the same idea here," said Timothy. "We understand that everything is thought and it's as simple for us to manifest a castle on the hill as it is for you to add two plus two in your head."

Matthew said, "If it's so easy to manifest everything, why don't you live in a castle with servants?"

"I've done that already and most people do that when they first come here," said Timothy. "But just imagine. When you can have anything and everything you want it all gets a little boring after awhile. So, eventually, people try different things, different jobs, just in order to learn things about themselves, stimulate their minds. That sort of thing.

"You get over the 'self-serving' thing pretty quickly because you can already have whatever you want. So, we get a cheap thrill by doing things for others!" said Timothy, smiling as he handed Amelia her portrait.

Amelia was surprised to see that it wasn't a picture of her face at all. Instead it was an exquisite collage of images. A fairy kingdom, trees, flowers, unicorns, desert canyons, mountains, the ocean with dolphins, and angels of light floating in a sky with stars and planets, the sun and moon. Gold was sprinkled over the entire painting like fairy dust.

"This is beautiful!" she exclaimed.

"It's called a 'soul' painting. It's a picture of you 'inside'," he said smiling.

Amelia smiled and said, "You know, I never even introduced myself. My name's . . . "

"Amelia," said Timothy. "And you're Matthew."

Matthew laughed and said, "How do you know that?"

"The universe isn't really as big a place as you think it is," he said with a wink as he began putting away paints and rummaging through his bag for some other things.

"No, really," said Matthew. "Did someone tell you we'd be here?"

"Oh, no," said Timothy. "I recognized you."

"Recognized us?" asked Matthew.

"Do you understand that light has different vibrations and wavelengths?" said Timothy.

"Yes," said Matthew.

"So, you see light vibrating at a certain speed and you call it green or blue or pink. And in the same way, your body has a vibration that's unique to you. No other person or thing in the universe has your exact vibration in that no two snowflakes or grains of sand are identical. There's this energy-field in you and around you and this field of energy can be read like a book. Or, more specifically, an autobiography, and your name's right on the cover. You've sometimes seen this energy field as light around another person, haven't you?" said Timothy.

"We both have," said Matthew.

"The fact is that even though you think you're solid, you're actually pure light," said Timothy. He turned to look at Matthew. "You're not quite with me are you?" He then looked at Amelia and said, "Amelia has had the *feeling* of being light but she doesn't quite understand the logic." He paused. "Matthew, you're the physics man, are you not?"

"Yes . . . " said Matthew, still unsure how Timothy knew these things.

"And you're familiar with quantum physics?" said Timothy.

"It's sort of a hobby of mine. They don't teach it in high school," said Matthew.

"Let's start with some very basic physics concepts so Amelia can stay with us. Let's look at your physical senses. What do they tell you about the world? What are some views out of history that we now know to be false?"

Amelia said, "The world is flat and stationary."

"The earth is the center of the universe," said Matthew, "with the sun, planets and stars revolving around it."

"Good," said Timothy. "Those were visually obvious *facts* a few hundred years ago. But even when science began to prove that those facts were false, it took a long time for the truth to become common knowledge. There was a lot of superstition but today anyone who doesn't know that the earth is round, rotates, and hurtles through space as it orbits around the sun would be considered ignorant. So, what do your senses tell you about your body?"

"That we're solid," said Amelia.

"Is that true according to quantum physics, Matthew?" asked Timothy.

"Not really," said Matthew.

"Wait, I have a question," said Amelia. "What does quantum mean?"

"Well, quantum would mean the smallest unit of something," said Matthew. "A quantum unit of electricity would be an electron; a quantum unit of light is a photon; gravity would be a graviton. So quantum physics looks at everything sort of from the inside out. More like inner-space exploration."

"So let's start from the 'inside,'" said Timothy. "What does an atom look like?"

"It has a nucleus, which is the only solid part of the atom," said Matthew, "and there are electrons. They're almost pure energy and they whiz around the nucleus at lightning speed. In the space between the nucleus and the electrons are subatomic particles: protons, electrons, quarks, leptons, bosons . . . ."

"That works, but let me add a little 'color' to that description!" said Timothy as he held his paintbrush dramatically in the air. "Amelia, let me give you an idea of the size of the nucleus. If you took all the nuclei of every person on the planet and put them together it would be about the size of a single grain of rice. If you took the nuclei of the entire planet, and put them all together, it would be the size of a sugar cube! And the distance from the nucleus to the electrons is proportionately the same distance as from the earth to the stars. So what appears to be a 'solid' body is in fact 99.9999% empty space."

"That's amazing!" cried Amelia.

"What's strange," said Matthew, "is that out of that 'emptiness' come nonmaterial particles."

"How can something be a particle and not made up of matter?" said Amelia.

"These particles are subatomic. They're so small you can't even see them," said Matthew.

"Then how do you know they exist?" asked Amelia.

"Because they leave behind trails," said Matthew.

"And to make this even more interesting," said Timothy, "these subatomic particles only come into existence through observation. They disappear when they're not being observed."

"Wouldn't you have to be observing them to know that they disappear when they're unobserved?" said Amelia.

"It isn't that they literally disappear; it's more that these particles shift into a different state," said Timothy. "You see, each particle is also a wave."

"Hold it!" said Amelia, "How can a particle be a wave?"

"It's a wave *until it's observed;* then it becomes a particle," said Timothy. "The important point, though, is that it can be seen as a wave *or* a particle, but not as both at the same time. So the particle is *created* by the fact that we're observing it."

"We create something simply by looking at it?" exclaimed Amelia.

"It's even more than that," said Timothy. "It's how you *choose to observe.* Remember I said you could see these subatomic particles as waves or particles, not both at once. In other words, it is the *conscious choice* to see a wave as a particle that brings it into existence. Are you still with me, Amelia?"

"No. I can't even imagine a wave being a particle!"

"Just trust that it's a proven fact in quantum physics. Don't worry whether or not you can figure it out," said Timothy.

"What are these subatomic particles made of?" said Amelia.

"Actually," said Matthew, "they're pure energy."

"That 'energy' is thought-force," said Timothy. "In a word, *Consciousness.*"

"Wait! Hold it! You're losing me," said Amelia. "I understood everything up to the part where the particles are pure energy. You lost me when you jumped to thought-force and consciousness. Where does the thought come from if it's not coming from my brain?"

"Are you the thought or the thinker, Amelia?" asked Timothy.

"I'm the thinker," she said.

"So you are not your mind or your body. You are the one who has the mind, the one who has the body. Doesn't that imply consciousness? Therefore consciousness is the foundation of mind and body."

"Isn't it the other way around? Isn't it that my mind and body create a place for me to be conscious?" said Amelia.

"Let's take a look at your mind and body, what really *is*, not the appearance. In the same way that the earth is not stationary and flat, the body is not static and solid. Did you know that 98% of the atoms in your body are replaced every year? You have a new brain every year; your skeleton is replaced every three months; your liver every six weeks; your skin every month. Every time you breathe, you're breathing out particles of yourself and breathing in particles of the entire universe. So, Amelia, this brain you have? It wasn't here last year. And the brain from last year wasn't here the year before."

"Are you saying we don't use our brain to think?" said Amelia.

"Let's say that the cells in the brain are like little floppy disks. You put information in on the computer and save it on your disks. As you go along you throw out the old disks and replace them with new disks. The new disks won't carry the information on the old disks unless you transfer the information."

"So how do you transfer the information?" said Amelia.

"By whatever you're thinking. You're the programmer. You're the thinker, not the thought," said

Timothy. "Remember the statement, 'I think. Therefore, I am'? The reason all the information seems to be the same is because of the 60,000 thoughts you think every day, 95% of those same thoughts you'll think tomorrow, except maybe in your case, since the two of you are on the 'accelerated program,' you might have a lower percentage rating!"

Amelia sighed, "I thought I was getting it but now I'm lost again."

"Are you still with me, Matthew?" said Timothy.

"I'm hanging in there. I've never put all of this information together in quite this way before. But I do know what you're talking about," he said.

"Let's go back to this 99.9999% space. What do scientists call this space?"

"The unified field," said Matthew.

"Why?" asked Timothy.

"Let me think about this for a minute," Matthew replied. "'Unified' means to bring together, to become one and, in the broadest sense, it would represent the universe. The word 'field' has to do with an interest, maybe even gaining knowledge. I guess you could call it Universal Intelligence. Ha! I never thought of it that way before."

"Good!" said Timothy. "Let's take it a little further. The word 'unify' literally means 'to form into one.' And 'field,' as you said, has to do with interest, which would imply thought or ideas. So the idea of unified field would literally have to do with the idea of consciousness being expressed as *form*."

"Would you say that again?" said Amelia.

"Don't worry, I'll explain this further," said Timothy, "but simply put, we're not bodies that have learned how to think and be intelligent. We are intelligence, consciousness, thought-force, that has learned how to create a body."

Amelia was stunned. She'd never heard of this before. She understood how people must have felt when they were first told the world was round. It was almost unbelievable and yet there was so much logic at the same time.

"So here's how it works," said Timothy. "You have an experience. You interpret the experience by how you choose to think about it and, according to what you think, your body produces chemicals that send messages to the body. Let me demonstrate!"

Suddenly Amelia and Matthew found themselves in pitch black on their way to the top of a roller coaster ride in the first car.

"Amelia!" yelled Matthew. "This is awesome! It's the 'E' ticket!"

"Oh God . . . !" screamed Amelia. "I hate roller coasters! They make me sick!"

As they plummeted down the other side Matthew threw his arms up in the air while Amelia, with her eyes shut tight, gripped the bar with white knuckles and held her breath to keep from screaming. Adrenaline pumped through her veins as she felt herself on the verge of becoming physically ill. Mercifully, the ride came to a halt just in time and she found herself back in the park sitting on the chair as if she'd never left except for the glaring fact that she was still shaky and weak.

"That was incredible!" shouted Matthew. "Can we do it again? That was absolutely the best roller coaster ride I've ever been on!"

"Take him, not me," said Amelia quickly.

"Sorry about that, Amelia," said Timothy, "but sometimes experience is the best teacher."

"What do you mean?" said Amelia, still a bit shaken.

"I wanted you to see for yourself how the mind and body are connected," said Timothy. "How do you both feel right now?"

Matthew said, "I feel incredible."

"Shaky and nervous," said Amelia weakly.

"Notice. You both had the exact same experience," said Timothy, "yet you each experienced an opposite physical and mental reaction. The reason is that your mind and body create powerful chemicals in response to whatever it is you're thinking or feeling. If you *feel* that a roller coaster ride is fun then your body will create chemicals more powerful than heroin: A good time with no side effects! If you're 'scared-to-death' then your body will create harmful chemicals . . . to the point that if you stayed in a place where you feared for your life long enough your body would produce enough harmful chemicals to literally kill you."

Amelia said, "I don't mean to interrupt, Timothy, but I'm not exactly sure how all of this applies to us. I mean, we've been traveling through time and dimensions and learning quantum physics but I don't know that I understand the point. It's all very interesting but what are we supposed to do with all this information when we get back home?"

"What you *do* with the information will be your choice," said Timothy. "Having the information will give you a choice. You've heard the phrase 'knowledge is power.' It's through the knowledge of what's real that you'll be able to identify the illusion. If you were planning to fly around the world who would you want as a pilot? Someone who understood physics and aerodynamics or someone who was convinced the world's flat? And if you knew you were going to have to fly your own plane someday, wouldn't you want to understand everything you could? It's impossible to know what the exact weather conditions will be but you know there *will* be weather, so you try to be prepared for everything and then learn through experience. I can't tell you exactly what's going to happen to you in the future but I can say that if I were you I'd pay attention as if my life depended on it."

Chills ran through Amelia's body. Somehow she had the feeling that Timothy knew something about the future but wasn't telling. Äsha knew something too. Why wouldn't they just tell her what they knew?

"Okay," said Amelia, "you have my full, undivided attention."

"Just trust," said Timothy. "The pieces will all fall into place. Sometimes you need a little perspective to understand. Just be patient."

"My brain's being overloaded," said Amelia. "I feel like I'm going to sink before I finish learning how to swim!"

Timothy continued. "I'd like to tell you both about an experiment. A scientist injected mice with a chemical that stimulated the immune system and at the same time the mice would smell camphor. Later, just the smell of camphor would cause the mice to produce chemicals within their own bodies that stimulated their immune systems. Another group of mice was injected with chemicals that would destroy the immune system and at the same time they also smelled camphor. Later, they would smell camphor and their bodies would produce chemicals that would destroy their immune system. So now you have two groups of mice: one group smells camphor and stays strong and healthy despite being exposed to germs and disease; the other group smells camphor and with the least provocation becomes ill and dies.

"Now, here's the point. What determined 'life or death' for the mice was the *memory* of camphor. It was the mind's interpretation that became a cellular memory."

"What do you mean," asked Amelia, "a cellular memory?"

"The memory wasn't in the brain," said Timothy. "The body carried the memory. Just as your body carried the memory of how you felt about roller coasters. You started feeling sick before anything had even happened."

"Can you put all this together for us?" said Matthew.

"Here it is: You are consciousness. What you call your mind and body is consciousness taking form. Unified field: Unified means form; field means interest, thought. Unified field, then, is thought taking form, and this thought-form shows up as your body."

"Then do we have access to Universal Consciousness?" said Matthew.

"You not only have access, you're a part of Universal Consciousness," Timothy said.

"I'm sorry. You've lost me again," said Amelia.

"If you live near a beach," said Timothy, "you have access to the ocean. If you are a wave, you're part of the ocean. Do you see?"

"This 99.9999% empty space is actually full of intelligence and because it isn't in form yet it's also full of potential," said Timothy. "So, you *are* that unlimited intelligence and you *are* that unlimited potential. But you must be conscious of this power to use it."

"I don't mean to seem dense," said Amelia, "but how do you make that potential real?"

"Thought," said Timothy. "Whatever you can imagine you can create as experience through the power of your own consciousness."

"But wait," said Amelia. "I can imagine walking through that brick wall over there but I can't actually do it."

"The only reason you 'can't' walk through that wall," said Timothy, "is because your belief, your conviction, that it's impossible is stronger than your belief that it is possible. You can't because you said so, not because of what is. The *fact* is that things are thoughts, and that brick wall is nothing more than an idea. Look at it, it's a particle; it has material form. Look away, it becomes a thought; it goes back to being a wave in the unified field. Could you walk through the wall in your mind?"

"Yes," said Amelia.

"That's because the wall has become subjective. It's a part of you; you're a part of it. When you observe the wall, it becomes objective: *It* does not change; your perception is what changes. Suddenly you see the wall as outside of yourself instead of inside. Notice you cannot see it as both outside and inside at the same time. You are either choosing to see a wave *or* a particle: Mind or Matter. When you see that the wave and the particle are not separate entities, they're one; then you'll see that things are thoughts."

Timothy stood up and walked right through the brick wall. When he returned he said, "And one other thing: Impossibilities never occur!"

Chapter IX

Interrupting the Program

Amelia just stared. She knew she had at least a working knowledge of what Timothy just said but she had a hard time believing what she was seeing. Timothy walked back and sat down as if what he'd done wasn't at all unusual.

"Now, the trick you must both learn is how to change your mind about what you see. Learn how to shift your perception. When you understand that things are thoughts you'll no longer be afraid of anything because you can always change your thinking. When your thinking changes, your experience will change, too."

Matthew suddenly jumped off his seat in total panic. A long, black snake had slithered up the back of the park bench and was sunning itself on the seat. Matthew's heart was pounding.

Timothy said, "How do you feel about snakes?"

"I hate snakes!" gasped Matthew.

Timothy nodded his head and said, "Do you want to change the way you feel?"

"You have no idea," said Matthew. "I went camping once and woke up with a rattlesnake in my

Children of Light

sleeping bag. I had to wait all day without moving a muscle for the snake to finally leave my bag."

Timothy laughed and said, "This is too perfect! Okay, Matthew. Walk over to that snake." Matthew was still visibly shaken.

"No," he said. "I can't."

Suddenly, Timothy threw a glass of water at Matthew. Shocked, Matthew instantly turned to Timothy and said, "What was that for?"

"Oh, nothing," said Timothy. "Go ahead. Walk over to that snake."

Matthew had temporarily forgotten about the snake but as he thought about it again his fear instantly returned. He knees were quivering and he simply shook his head. Suddenly he was hit by another glass of water. He stopped and stared at Timothy. "What are you doing? Are you crazy?"

Timothy shrugged his shoulders and said, "Go ahead. Walk over to that snake."

Once again Matthew felt the fear creeping back. His breathing became shallow, his heart was again pounding when suddenly WHAM! Timothy dumped an entire bucket of water over Matthew's head. Matthew whirled around to see Amelia valiantly trying not to laugh and Timothy doing his best to keep a straight face.

Matthew burst out laughing and said, "This is ridiculous!" With that he walked right up to the snake, plucked it off the bench, held it out to Timothy and said, "Here. Does this make you happy?"

Interrupting the Program

Timothy smiled and said, "Does it make *you* happy?"

Matthew thoughtfully set the snake on the ground next to a tree and said, "How did you do that?"

"Well," said Timothy, "it's really quite simple. The biological computer you call your brain was programmed to think fear and panic around snakes the same way the mice were programmed to react to the smell of camphor . . . and the way Amelia reacts to roller coasters. I simply *interrupted* the program by pouring water on you. You felt surprise, annoyance and, finally, laughter. So now, with laughter being your last 'computer entry,' whenever you see a snake you'll probably laugh, remembering a bucket of water being dumped on your head. So, if you want to change your mind about the way you're thinking or feeling, you simply interrupt the way you're thinking."

Matthew said, "Do I have to have water dumped on my head every time."

Timothy laughed and said, "That would probably work, but I think I'll let the two of you figure it out for yourselves. Remember, 95% of what you think today you thought yesterday. It's like a record you play over and over. But if you scratched the record several times so that it sounded like a series of pops and scrapes it wouldn't take long for you to stop listening. If you want to change your experience you have to change what you're thinking. Learn to interrupt negative thought patterns. Just remember: Everything's choice. So what are you choosing?" With that, Timothy instantly disappeared.

"Matthew," said Amelia, "why do these people disappear every time I start to understand what they're talking about?"

Smiling, Matthew shook his head and said, "I don't know Amelia. Maybe they just know when we've heard enough. I mean this is a lot to absorb."

They walked along quietly and headed back to their hotel. Just before they reached the building Amelia said, "Do you think Äsha will be able to find us? I wonder if she knows we're here?"

"I think she does, Amelia. Look!"

There was Äsha standing at the end of the street, smiling at them. Next to her were two beautiful Arabian horses. One was a bay with white stockings and a star on his forehead. The other was dapple grey with a long mane and a tail that swept the ground. Next to them was a roly-poly, white pony. None of the horses had bridles or saddles and they stood there calmly. When they reached Äsha she showed them their horses.

Although Amelia had ridden horses before she was scared to get on without a bridle or saddle. However, to admit she was afraid might have given Matthew the opportunity to "interrupt" her bio-computer programming and she definitely preferred to ride with dry clothing, so she stood up straight, took a deep breath and pretended to be quite nonchalant about the whole thing.

Matthew helped Amelia get on Morning Glory, the dapple grey, and he effortlessly jumped on Sky while Äsha sat astride Breezy the pony. Amelia wondered where they would ride and how they'd tell their horses where to go but before she could ask any questions they were all riding through an Alpine meadow.

At first Amelia thought it would be frightening to ride an unfamiliar horse, especially without a saddle, but Morning Glory moved as smoothly as a big rocking horse. Matthew smiled and laughed as he and Sky sailed easily across the meadow. Despite Breezy's short legs, he kept up the pace quite admirably and Äsha joyously threw her arms in the air embracing the wind.

The pony and horses seemed to move in one accord as if they all knew exactly where they were and where they were supposed to go. Amelia had finally grown accustomed to things she didn't understand so she just enjoyed the ride and the scenery. A moment ago it was springtime but here, wherever it was, they were in the midst of autumn.

It was a warm, Indian summer day and the colors were more bright and clear than anything Amelia could remember. Translucent yellow aspens stood alongside maples dressed in fire engine red and ancient oaks looked as if their leaves had been painted with real gold. The fir and pine trees added fragrance and a variety of color. There wasn't a cloud in the sky and the sun lit up the meadow with it's bright green grass, flaming sumac and softly muted dried plants and flowers.

All at once the horses and pony slowed down and came to a halt. Äsha slid off her pony and motioned for Matthew and Amelia to join her. Äsha smiled at them and said, "At the top of the trail you see there along the stream is a cave. You're both to go to the cave."

"Aren't you coming with us?" said Amelia.

"I'll wait here for you," said Äsha.

The truth was that Amelia didn't really like caves and would very much have preferred Äsha along for protection but at least Matthew was with her and that made it a lot easier. As they walked up the hill she had the strangest feeling that something was going to happen, something that would most likely be unpleasant.

The trail curved and dipped over the edge of a hill and all at once they were at the cave. They both stopped short as they saw an old gypsy woman sitting at the mouth of the cave in front of a fire. She was dressed in a peasant blouse with a long, full skirt, and a scarf around her head, and she was wearing rings with large jewels and crystal necklaces. She sat at a table with two extra chairs.

"Ah! Here you are!" she said, smiling, with a thick Russian accent.

"Were you expecting us?" said Amelia.

"Vhy do you t'ink I'm here?" she said.

"I don't know," laughed Amelia. "We're not even sure why we're here!"

"Come sit down! I'm here to teach you about superstition. Do you think I did a good job of dressing the part?" she said as she made a few adjustments.

Amelia and Matthew both laughed. He said, "I think you're perfect."

"The accent's not too much, is it?" she said earnestly in an unmistakably Bronx accent.

They both tried to keep a straight face. "Oh, no. It's a great accent," said Amelia enthusiastically.

"Ah dat's vonderful!" said Anna, returning to her original Russian accent. "Vell, good. Let the games begeen!" She laid cards out on the table. "Oh, forgive me. I forgot to introduce myself. I'm Anna." She looked at Amelia and winked. "We have a lot of 'A' names floating around here, don't you think? 'A's are very good! Excellent vibration!"

Amelia liked Anna. She seemed like a grown-up elf. She was also thoroughly enjoying the fact that Anna couldn't quite keep her accent straight. The image was something between a nice, old Jewish lady from the Bronx and a gypsy from the Ukraine. Anna proceeded to reach into a huge, purple velvet bag. It seemed to be empty but all kinds of things kept materializing: candles, incense, a crystal ball wrapped in silk, more cards, a small velvet bag with what appeared to be stones, some Tibetan bells and a few charts and one great big book. The title took up the entire cover of the book, it read: "Esoteric 101: A Beginner's Guide. Palmistry, Astrology, Numerology, Lexigrams, Tarot Reading, Tea Leaf Reading, Russian Gypsy Fortune Telling." In smaller words below the title it said "With a special manual covering subjects such as: Why You Came Here, Where You're Going (and the ever popular) How to Get Back to Where You Came From If You Think You Made a Mistake and Took the Wrong Fork in the Road." Then Amelia noticed the author: "Anna-stasia Lebowitz-Kowalski-Smith-Smith-Goldberg-Rosen-Speillberg."

Anna noticed Amelia staring at the book. "I've been married several times and twice to him, the only non-Jew, but still a good man," she said pointing to 'Smith'. "I wanted them all to have credit," she added, shrugging her shoulders. Anna finished spreading everything nicely out over the table. "In a word, what do you both see before you?"

Amelia was puzzled. She couldn't think of one word to describe all of the things on the table. She had never known a gypsy or a psychic and she'd been taught by her mother that there wasn't much in it, just a bunch of old wives tales according to her mom. On the other side of the coin was Amelia's great-aunt Nell. Amelia's dad called her a "Born-Again-Bible-Thumper." Aunt Nell said that psychics, tarot cards, crystal balls and the like were "of the devil" and anyone who did such things was "working for Satan." Looking at Anna with her big smile, round face and happy eyes made that concept a little hard to swallow.

"Do you give up?" said Anna. Matthew and Amelia nodded. "Tools!" she exclaimed, clapping her hands together proudly. "They're tools of the trade! So, what do you think? No, I take that back," she said. "What have you been taught?"

Amelia told her a little about her mom's philosophy and added a few colorful tidbits about Aunt Nell. Anna smiled as she listened, enthusiastically nodding her head.

"My dear children," she said. "There is nothing inherently good or bad in anything: *Intention* is everything. Of course there's something to be said for interpretation, too, but that's another subject!"

"Intention?" said Matthew.

"Of course," said Anna. "A hammer is an instrument. You can use it to put up a picture or you can knock someone over the head. An instrument has no power. It can be used for a good purpose or a bad one. It's the intention behind it!"

"Do you believe in all these things?" said Amelia, indicating everything that was laid out on the table.

Anna said, "Amelia, my dear, whatever you believe is true for you. Yes?"

"Yes . . . " said Amelia hesitantly, thinking for a moment.

Anna leaned close to Amelia and said confidentially, in her usual Bronx accent, "I have no idea whether all of this is true. I just like to be entertained and these are *entertaining* beliefs." She winked at her and said, "Cards, numerology, astrology. They all entertain me! Not to mention the people who end up sitting across from me at the table!"

Anna spread out 88 cards face down on the table. She looked at Amelia and said, "Go ahead. Pick out six cards and put them face-up on the table. Don't worry, they're just pictures. Nothing will jump out and bite you."

Amelia picked a picture of an angel with long, blonde hair, sitting by a pond, dipping her toe into the water. The next picture was a sword being held up in the light, pointing toward the sky. The third picture was a fountain with a young man and woman facing each other, holding hands. The next was a bird soaring alone in the sky. The fifth picture was a snake in the grass and the last was the sun rising over the ocean.

"So, Amelia, vhat do you see?" said Anna, the Russian accent returning.

"I don't know. It doesn't really make sense to me," said Amelia.

"Dees ees your fearst time. I'll help you," said Anna. "The angel is, of course, you, my angel. The water represents emotion. The man and the woman represent romantic love and, since the angel is dipping her toe in the water, I'd say that you're falling in love; not quite ready to dive in, but happy to test the water. Yes?"

Amelia could feel herself blushing. She put her head in her hand and started to laugh. Without looking up she said, "Yes."

"It is okay, my pretty child," said Anna, smiling. "There is nothing new here for Matthew either. Let's see what else is here before us. A sword card between the angel and the lovers. The sword represents clarity. You are not someone to just fall head over heels in love, my dear. You must be clear headed and a man must appeal to your mind as well as your heart. The bird means that you must also feel that you have the freedom to be yourself. You would never be happy playing a role that's not you. Does this all make sense to you so far?"

Amelia shook her head and smiled. "That's me exactly!"

"Now, this snake in the grass," Anna said. "I believe this is in your future. You will be dealing with a very subtle, intelligent, yet poisonous mind; someone who's very deceptive. But look at this last card with the sun over the ocean. This represents you rising above the sea of emotion, having perspective, maintaining your own power."

"Can I see what the other cards look like?" said Amelia.

"Of course," said Anna, scooping up the cards and handing them to Amelia.

Amelia looked at the images on the cards and there really weren't any other cards that came even close to depicting her current situation and feelings.

"I don't understand," said Amelia. "How does this work? I just randomly picked those cards. Of course, I don't know about the future but the other cards were perfectly accurate."

"Here's my theory. I made this up all by myself!" she said with a wink. "Suppose you had a dream, Amelia, and you went to your mother and she helped you analyze the dream. Everything would have meaning. Yes?"

"Of course," said Amelia.

"Why?" said Anna.

"Because everything in a dream is coming out of your subconscious," Amelia replied.

"So, if you dreamed you were playing cards and you got the 2 of Hearts, it could mean you were in love.

It wouldn't just be a coincidence; it would have meaning. Then let's say while you were playing cards you dreamed you saw a snake and you were frightened. It might mean you were scared of falling in love. Your subconscious mind would be directly mirroring whatever was happening in your life. The only trick would be understanding how to interpret the dream. Do you both understand that your mind is creating *this* reality as well as your dream world?"

"Almost . . . ." said Matthew.

"Well you understand the unified field. You know that things are thoughts. In the same way that *you are consciousness* which has learned how to create a body, this same consciousness has in fact learned how to create an entire world! You do it every night when you dream. Why not during the day?! So, Amelia, when you turn over a card there is nothing random or coincidental. Your mind already knows what it wants to reveal to you. You see what your mind wants to communicate to you. This is how you've learned to teach yourself. You're both student and teacher. Even *I* am just *you* teaching yourself!"

"Oh, no!" said Amelia, slumping down in her chair. "I was just starting to catch on until you said that: 'You are me, teaching myself.'"

"Amelia, you keep forgetting," said Anna patiently. "There's *nothing* outside of yourself. When you dream every person in your dream is an aspect of you. It's the same thing. You dream about your mother. It's the 'mother' part of yourself and your 'mother' will show up as either nurturing or judgmental depending on how *you* are seeing yourself. In 'real' life it's exactly the same thing. If you're feeling loving toward yourself then your mother will show up as loving. And if your mom is being judgmental then she is most likely mirroring some judgment you have of yourself."

"Hold it!" said Matthew, his face beaming. "I think I at least understand the concept. Okay, let me see if I can actually say this: There can't be anyone 'outside' because the unified field means literally one-thought."

"Wait!" said Amelia. "I'm sorry to interrupt, but when you said 'one-thought' I just saw in my mind, written in huge, gold letters 'THE WORD.' What does that mean?"

Anna smiled, "I almost don't want to say this because there are certain words that 'trigger' people and make it difficult for them to learn. However, Amelia, since I just got done telling you that there are no coincidences, I'm going to trust that you'll both be able to hear this. Have you ever read the first paragraph of the Old Testament?"

"No," said Amelia.

"It says, 'In the beginning was the Word, and the Word was with God, and the Word was God," said Anna. "The word 'beginning' in its original translation meant 'only.' If this is your 'only' chance, it means 'now'. So the opening would read: 'In the *now* was the Word. What would 'The Word' be? One-thought, Universal Consciousness. Then it says 'The Word was God.' So, God is then it just goes on to say how infinitely creative this Universal Intelligence is. And I guess you could say that history is a record of how this Consciousness has been teaching itself."

"But so many tragic things have happened in our history," said Amelia. "Why would this Intelligence choose so much pain?"

"The pain, the tragedy . . . . It's not real, Amelia," said Anna. "Remember, darkness is the *absence* of light. In and of itself it has no power, no reality. You can't measure darkness. It has no qualities or characteristics of its own. If you have to walk through a dark basement, are you battling the dark or dealing with your own *fear* of the dark?"

"My own fear," said Amelia.

"What was your last, big fear of the dark?" asked Anna.

"When Matthew and I were out in the desert and couldn't see to get back," she replied.

"And what were you afraid of?"

"That we'd die."

"Did you?"

"To be honest, I'm not sure," said Amelia.

"Well, you're here, aren't you!" said Anna, laughing and throwing up her arms.

Amelia laughed, "You've got a point! 'I think. Therefore I am.'"

"Or, better yet," said Anna, "I AM. Therefore, I think!

"While you're releasing judgments, let go of the one around death. Death doesn't exist. It's just a part of the illusion. When you recognize that something's a dream, an illusion, do you spend a lot of time worrying about it? Or do you think, 'Hmm, that was interesting. I wonder what that meant?' and then get on with your day?"

"If it's not real," said Amelia, "then what's the purpose?"

"You learn through contrast. You learn through opposition. Without the experience of hate would you really appreciate love? If everything were light and love and angels it might be nice for a while, but where's the challenge? Where's the opportunity to exercise your own free will, to think creatively in the face of a crisis? There would be no choices!"

"So are you saying that darkness and evil are good?" said Matthew.

"I would say that good and evil, light and dark, right and wrong, are judgments," said Anna. "'Thinking makes it so.' It's not necessary to judge. Being judgmental takes away your power to think creatively because you give your power over to whatever it is you're judging."

"If you're not judging a situation or a person then doesn't that mean you'd just stand by and watch someone being robbed or killed?" asked Matthew.

"Let me put it simply," Anna replied. "If there's action to be taken and you *feel* you can make a difference, do it. If the situation is out of your hands, say to yourself, 'This is none of my business.'"

"None of my business? Why?" said Matthew.

"This isn't an excuse for apathy, Matthew," said Anna, "but if there's nothing you can *do*, then holding negative thoughts around the situation will only draw more negativity because whatever you're thinking, you experience. If you're really mad at someone, how do you feel?"

"Sick to my stomach."

"Does being sick to your stomach change the situation or the other person?" she asked.

"No."

"It's your body literally saying to you, 'I can't stomach it when you're angry.' So, saying 'this is none of my business' neutralizes your feelings," said Anna. "It takes you out of negativity and removes you from the realm of judgment. Got it?"

"Just about," he said.

"Remember the psychiatrist in India trying to force his way through the 'boulders'? He had to neutralize the negativity in his mind *first*. There was no outside force-field stopping him. He was literally running into his own negative thought patterns."

"Okay," said Matthew.

Interrupting the Program

Anna stopped and stared at her crystal ball. Then she looked at Amelia. This was the first time Amelia had seen Anna with a serious look.

"My dear, "I'm a bit torn as to whether I should tell you this."

"What? Tell me what?" said Amelia.

"I've just seen a bit of your future. Of course, no future is set in stone but this apparently is a future that you've chosen and you're working your way toward it."

"What do you see?" asked Amelia urgently.

"I see you in a prison cell, all alone in the dark," said Anna.

"You mean as an adult? I'm going to end up in prison?"

"No. This will happen very soon."

"But what could I possibly do to end up in prison? For one thing, I'm too young!"

"This is not a regular prison. You're more of a captive; seems to me kidnapped," said Anna. "My dear, I don't know why you've chosen this or what it is you're there to do, but be sure before you leave Äsha that you *understand* everything. Don't wait to ask questions. Make sure you're clear."

Anna vanished but Amelia could hear Anna's last words even though she could no longer see her: "Remember who you are! Remember!"

Chapter X

The Crystal Cave

Everything was gone except the chairs Matthew and Amelia were sitting on. When they stood up, those disappeared too.

Matthew said, "I guess we should go back."

"Wait," said Amelia, closing her eyes. "I have the feeling we're supposed to go in the cave."

"We don't have a flashlight," said Matthew.

"I know, but we're still supposed to go in."

Matthew took a deep breath. "Okay. Do you think this is a test or something?" he asked.

"I have no idea."

They both stepped into the cave rather cautiously. The cave was cool and moist with a rather large entrance. They headed toward the back and found a passage that turned sharply and sloped downward. They were surprised to see that on the ceiling above were crystals emanating just enough light for them to see. They walked along the passage until they came to a large chamber with a low ceiling. The entire ceiling was filled with all different colors of crystals lit from within.

Matthew reached up to touch a red crystal and it fell right into his hand. As he held it the crystal began glowing intensely and all the other crystals went dark. Suddenly Matthew and Amelia found themselves in the midst of a hologram. They were standing in a magnificent foyer of a mansion. There were crystal chandeliers, beautiful antiques, exquisite porcelain vases, and sculptures. In the midst of everything a six year old boy was sitting forlornly on a large trunk with his hands folded on his lap and his ankles crossed. He was dressed in a navy blue school uniform with a cap.

"That's my father when he was a boy!" exclaimed Matthew.

A heavy-set black maid rushed into the room with the butler and a gardener. She said to them, "Quick! Get his trunk out of here before she sees it." The boy jumped off as the men hoisted the trunk off the ground and headed up the stairs. At that moment the front door flew open. An incredibly beautiful woman, elegantly dressed in the height of fashion, breezed into the house followed by a chauffeur laden with shopping bags and boxes. She stopped for a moment, stared at the boy and yelled, "Bessie! What is this child doing here?"

"Well, Mrs. McKinley, your son has just returned from boarding school."

"I am perfectly aware of that, Bessie. But he was supposed to go to summer camp. Haven't you been informed?"

"Yes, I know that Missus, but the camp doesn't start for another two weeks."

"Oh, my gracious," said Mrs. McKinley. "Must I do everything myself? And tonight, of all nights, when we're having my niece's debutante ball! Certainly there must be a camp that starts earlier somewhere in the world! Bessie, tell my secretary to find a camp that's open. Immediately!"

"Yes, Mrs. McKinley."

"And Bessie, if that can't be accomplished, be sure you feed Matthew, Jr., in the kitchen while he's here. He's happier eating with the staff anyhow." She briefly looked in her son's direction again and said coolly, "Hello, dear. I hope you had fun at school this year. I'm sure you'll have a marvelous summer at camp. I must run now, my darling. Mommy has so much to do for the party tonight." She quickly bent down, gave him a peck on the cheek, turned and left the room. The boy just stood there, his lower lip quivering, tears filling his eyes, trying desperately not to cry.

"There, there, master Matthew," said Bessie, scooping the boy up in her arms. "Hush, now. You don't need to cry."

With that the boy burst into tears and said, "Why doesn't my mommy want me here? I try to be good and quiet."

"Oh, my precious lamb! There's no little boy in the world better than you. Maybe your mama just thinks you'd be happier in camp with children your own age." The boy looked at her with tear-stained cheeks, then looked down and shook his head slowly.

The hologram disappeared. The crystals in the ceiling lit up again but the crystal in Matthew's hand had gone dark so he slipped the crystal in his pocket.

He turned to Amelia and said, "My father never spoke of his mother. She died when I was two or three. All I know about Grandma is that when she died my father inherited everything since he was the only child. He sold every item that belonged to her. Of course, he kept the house because it had been in the family."

"That's so sad," said Amelia. "I don't understand why she couldn't love him."

At that moment the crystal in his pocket began to glow. Instantly they were standing on a grassy meadow and a tall, thin, pale and sickly-looking man walked right up to Matthew.

Matthew whispered to Amelia, "It's my father!"

The man stood there looking at Matthew and finally said, "I'm so proud of you, Matthew. And I'm so sorry you don't know how much I love you." He held Matthew's gaze for a moment and then whispered, "I've been trapped. Please forgive me."

Then his father stepped back a few paces and turned into a stone statue. A moment later the stone began to crack. Suddenly, it split open revealing the same teary-eyed boy they had seen earlier dressed in a school uniform. The boy ran to Matthew and threw his arms around him. Matthew picked him up and said, "It's okay. I love you. I'll be your friend." With that, the little boy put his arms around Matthew's neck, kissed him, and said, "I love you."

Suddenly everything vanished. They were standing in the cave and the crystal had gone dark while the other crystals were lit again.

There were tears in Matthew's eyes as he looked at Amelia and said, "That couldn't have been a hologram! That was a real little boy in my arms. I could feel him breathing. I could even feel his heart beating. That was definitely my father as a little boy." He stopped for a moment and said quietly, "I don't understand."

As he said those words a light began to shimmer in the semi-darkness. They watched as it shifted and changed until it appeared as vibrant gold. From this color came a voice that said, "Stop trying to understand with your mind. True understanding is from the heart."

With that, a bright blue crystal dislodged itself from the ceiling and gently drifted down until it hovered right in front of Amelia. She held her hand out and the crystal dropped into her palm. She closed her hand and the light-energy from the crystal shot through her body. There was an intense blue light that radiated from her and again they heard the voice. It said, "The **Truth** is your power, Amelia."

Suddenly Amelia found herself wearing an elegant, purple velvet dress with a V-cut back, and stockings and heels. She had on make-up, earrings and a necklace. Her hair was curled and she looked like a homecoming queen. It was dusk and Amelia was totally alone in the midst of San Francisco in a park with homeless people. She knew she wasn't in a hologram. There were shanties constructed from plastic, cardboard, wood and shopping carts. Strange people drifted by her, shadows of former youth, forgotten innocence, bent from the gravity of life's burdens.

Amelia's heart pounded as she looked for Matthew or at least some meaning in what had just happened. She wanted to run, to find the security of a policeman. But then what? Could she simply explain she was from another dimension and just wanted to go back? Then she heard, "Listen." She looked around, but no one was there and the voice was not in her imagination. She heard it very distinctly.

There was nothing she could do and clearly no place to run so she sat down on a bench. As Amelia looked around she noticed that everyone had light around them but mostly the light was grayish with patches of black. It was a dense color, almost opaque.

She watched a large, black man in his mid-30's arguing with a white woman about the same age. She couldn't hear exactly what was being said but she watched as the surrounding energy moved back and forth. The colors around them were dark red, an ugly sulphurish yellow, and black. It appeared at first that they were both trying to intimidate each other, arguing louder and louder.

Finally, the woman pulled a large knife out of her bag but before she could use it the man struck her with such force that she spun around and slid across the pavement. He kicked her repeatedly as she begged and pleaded for him to stop.

Amelia was horrified. There was nothing she could do and no one else to intercede. Then she saw a golden light right in front of her, blocking her view of the man and woman. The voice was loving and gentle. It said, "See this man as perfect."

In her mind Amelia replied, "Perfect! Look at him! He's cruel and spiteful!"

"My dear, he is your mirror."

"What?!"

"He has forgotten who he is, even as you have forgotten who you are."

Amelia tried to grasp the meaning of this statement. She remembered Timothy saying, "You're the thinker, not the thought."

"That's it, Amelia," said the light. "See beyond the distortion of thought and action. Transform the violence and anger within yourself."

"But I'm not violent and angry," said Amelia. "I would never hurt someone like that!"

"Aren't you angry right now with that man?"

"Yes."

"It only takes a tiny spark to start a forest fire. Now, think with me for a moment," the Light said. "You look for guilt; I look for innocence. Look with me and see innocence."

Amelia struggled with the idea that this man was innocent. Clearly he was cruel and violent. Then she heard the voice again. It was totally loving, totally patient with her.

"Truth is your freedom and it's your gift to them."

For the first time Amelia looked through the golden light at the man. She saw his heart in front of her. Outside, there was steel-grey armor but she looked past that and saw his heart was bruised and bloody. Around his heart floated scenes from the man's past.

She saw him beaten repeatedly as a child. Then she watched in horror as his alcoholic mother pinned him to the floor, her knees on his arms and, with a carving knife, sliced his chest. She saw him depleted, with no control, and witnessed the energy around him being continually sucked away by his mother. Then she watched him get older and become determined that no one would ever hurt him again.

Suddenly the man's flesh and bones became transparent. Amelia could see "through" the man's body to a small boy inside finally big enough to fight back and totally unaware that this woman he was kicking was *not* his mother.

Then she turned her attention to the woman groveling on the ground. She could see the woman's heart through the golden light also. She saw an equally violent childhood very similar to the man's childhood. To her utter amazement Amelia saw that as a child the woman wanted so much to be loved she came to associate physical violence with love. She watched as the mother beat the little girl with a rubber hose. The child was saying to herself, "Mommy hits me because she loves me. Mommy just wants me to be a good girl." As the man repeatedly kicked her this "little girl" was saying, "I know he really loves me. If he didn't care he would just walk away."

Children of Light

Amelia thought, "It's a mistake! They're both making a mistake!" Then she remembered "helping" the psychiatrist in India and thought about how she might be able to help them in the same way. With the psychiatrist they had all visualized the way the cave was in reality. So who were these people in reality? What was the truth behind what she was seeing?

Suddenly the little boy and girl "stepped out" of the man and woman and walked up to Amelia. They began taking off their clothes. Amelia gasped and tears immediately came to her eyes as she saw the children covered with ugly scars and bruises all over their bodies. Even emotional wounds showed up on their flesh. Around their bodies was a grey energy of fear. Amelia cried, "Oh, you poor babies!"

The Light said, "You recognize the innocence of these little ones, that the scars were put there by someone else. Recognize the innocence of *all* your brothers and sisters."

Deep compassion filled Amelia's heart as she wept. The "children" crawled up in Amelia's lap. They felt real, yet Amelia had seen these children emerge from the people and walk through the golden light. She held them in her arms, kissed their cheeks, and said softly, "You're safe. You're safe! You're perfectly safe." She looked at them both with so much love and said, "There's a world you've never known. It's *full* of joy and love and freedom. I promise. It's there for you. Nobody can take it away from you. Nobody can touch *you*. Your body isn't you. These scars aren't you."

The Crystal Cave

"I was a bad girl," said the child.

"Oh, no!" said Amelia quickly. "You're not bad. You're a sweet, precious little girl and you deserve to be loved."

"My mommy loves me," said the girl.

"That's all your mommy understands about love," said Amelia, "but sweetheart, love's harmless. Your mommy just hasn't learned that yet. But I'll tell you how to feel love . . . if you'd like," she said, including the little boy. The children both nodded their heads.

"Close your eyes. No peeking. Think about the place where *you* are where nobody can touch you. Now imagine some place you like a lot, a place you'd like to go. Where are you?"

The little girl said happily, "I'm floating in the sky. I'm a bird, flying, flying, flying . . . ."

"I'm playing in the sand at the beach," said the boy, "and I'm all alone with my castle. Can I have a dog with me, too?" he said, peeking out of one eye.

"Sure," said Amelia. "This is a place you can always go to feel safe and loved. It's your special place and no one can be there unless you invite them. This is a place where you're always loved, always understood."

Amelia looked at the children on her lap with their eyes closed looking truly peaceful. Then she noticed the scars were dissolving on their bodies and she started crying again.

She felt she wasn't alone. She looked up and the man and woman were standing in front of her.

"Are you okay?" said the woman.

Amelia realized she had been talking out loud and crying through the whole thing. She dabbed her nose with the back of her hand. The woman reached into her bag and produced a wadded-up napkin. She looked at Amelia with concern and said, "It's kinda rumpled but it's clean. What's the matter?"

"Actually," said Amelia, "I was worried about you."

"Me?!" said the woman, surprised. "Oh! That over there with him? That was nothin'."

"Temporary insanity," said the man. He turned to the woman and said, "I am sorry, hon'."

"It's alright," she said, brushing it off as if it had been nothing. She looked back at Amelia with concern. "But what about you! One minute I thought he was gonna beat my brains out and the next thing I know he's staring at you sittin' here in the middle of this trashy park in your pretty velvet dress, crying your eyes out and talking to yourself!"

"Are you lost?" said the man as the park lights flickered on.

"Not really," said Amelia, blowing her nose with the napkin. She started laughing as she saw a mental picture of what they must have been seeing, complete with two "imaginary" children on her lap. Trying to keep a straight face she said, "Someone's meeting me here pretty soon. I'll be fine, thanks."

The Crystal Cave

"Listen, I gotta go to work," said the woman. "It ain't much of a job but it's work. Now, listen. You shouldn't be here alone. This isn't a safe place for a pretty, young girl in a party dress. Mike, you stay with her. Okay? Until her friend gets here."

"Yeah, alright," he said and sat down next to Amelia.

The woman looked at the man for a moment. He said, "I really am sorry, babe. You know I get a little crazy around knives."

She nodded and sighed, "I know. My fault. Don't let anything bad happen to her." She leaned over and whispered in Amelia's ear, "You saved my life you know, cryin' and dressed up for a party like you was." She smiled and patted Amelia's shoulder. "'Bye now." She waved and walked away.

Amelia had thought for sure a few moments earlier that the lesson was over and she'd be back with Matthew. But now she felt a bit panicked. What if she'd slipped into another dimension accidentally and no one could find her and she might never get back? Who was this man? It was one thing thinking about him from a distance, but now he was just a few inches away.

"So how ya doin'?" said the man.

"I'm fine . . . ." said Amelia.

Amelia had never met a black man before. She had been raised (as her father put it) in Wonder Bread City, a small town with virtually no ethnic minorities. She'd never thought of herself as prejudiced but she felt nervous sitting next to this man. And, oddly enough, he appeared to be a bit frightened of her, too. He didn't seem to know quite how to handle himself and came off with a lot of bravado.

He shifted uncomfortably on the bench and then said again, "So how ya doin'?"

She said, "I'm still okay."

Mike nodded his head and rocked back and forth a little until someone he knew walked up and said hello for a minute. When the friend left, Mike looked at Amelia again and said, "So how ya doin'?"

This time Amelia burst out laughing. The absurdity of this big man (he was 6'6"), whom she felt was most assuredly a drug dealer, being nervous around her was entirely too funny to suppress.

"You know," she laughed, "if you want this conversation to go anywhere, you're going to have to come up with something else."

The man laughed, slightly embarrassed. "Sorry," he said. "I don't know. Umm, well . . . . My name's Mike. What's yours?"

"Amelia," she said, sticking her hand out.

He shook her hand. "Nice to meet you. So what are you doin' here?" he said a bit suspiciously.

Amelia laughed. "That's a good question. Well, like I said, I'm supposed to meet someone here."

"This is a bad place for a young girl like you ta be waitin'."

The Crystal Cave

"It's okay," said Amelia. "I'm fine."

During this conversation Amelia found herself looking directly into the man's eyes. Had this happened before her experience of leaving the third dimension she would have barely looked at the man and probably would have gotten up to leave. But Anna's words, "There are *no* coincidences," echoed in her ears. She knew she was here to learn something and the lesson wasn't yet complete.

She heard the voice again, "As you perceive this man, so you will perceive yourself."

Amelia was confused. There was nothing remotely similar between them. Then she remembered Äsha quoting Shakespeare, "Nothing is either good or bad but *thinking* makes it so." She thought of how she'd perceived the "little boy" with so much compassion. She realized the "boy" was still inside the man and as she looked in the man's eyes she recognized the child she'd been holding on her lap. The expression on Amelia's face softened with this recognition and, in turn, Mike became more comfortable.

With genuine interest and concern Amelia said, "How do you survive here with no home?"

"It's pretty tough," said Mike. "The worst year, though, was when I first came here, when I was fourteen. I was from a family of thirteen kids. We lived in L.A. My dad, he was in prison the whole time. He spent a year in the hole."

"The hole?"

154

"That's where they put guys who murder somebody in jail. They lock 'em up and keep 'em in the dark for a year. There ain't even a toilet, just a hole in the floor."

Amelia had her full attention on Mike, listening carefully to everything he said.

He continued, "Well, anyhow, we was on welfare and I was the youngest. Actually, I had a twin brother but he died at birth. He was the 'good seed' and I was the 'bad seed.' At least that's what my momma a'ways said."

It was clear to Amelia that Mike didn't feel sorry for himself. He was just reciting a few facts from his own personal history. He wasn't looking for pity but clearly he liked Amelia's undivided attention. For half an hour he rambled on about his life and throughout the dialogue he'd refer to himself as the 'bad seed.'

Amelia listened, and the more she could feel herself being fine with where she was, not worried about what was going to happen, the happier she felt. The man and the "boy" began to blend together and she found herself genuinely caring about Mike, seeing him and understanding him in a way that would have been impossible prior to changing her view of him.

"Anyhow, things was bad at home. I was havin' ta stick up for my sisters when they was datin' guys. I got in a lot of fights, bein' the 'bad seed' an' all. And this one guy was gonna kill me. So I took off and came here. I been livin' on the streets eva since. Well, 'cep' one time I went square."

"Square?"

"Ya know. Got off drugs. Got a job. I even had my own apartment. Used to take homeless people in off the street but I hadda quit that 'cause they kep' rippin' me off."

Amelia looked Mike squarely in the eye and said, "Mike, I don't think you're a 'bad seed'. I just think you've never really had the opportunity to give."

Mike looked at Amelia and said genuinely, "You're like a diamond to me. You know that? Everything about you shines like the sun. You're like them pretty marigolds over there." He smiled, obviously enjoying that he'd come up with some good comparisons.

Amelia wondered when the last time was this man had someone talk to him who was genuinely interested in him. Or when did he last hear a compliment or something good about himself? She could hardly believe this man's transformation before her eyes. He went from being nervous and suspicious with all kinds of walls and barriers to a man who was gentle and thoughtful. She'd spoken from her heart. She had nothing to gain by being kind to him. Clearly, this had opened the way for him to be the same way.

Amelia could see that when she changed her perception of this man her fear disappeared. Until that moment she'd never really seen that her perception could profoundly touch and influence the other person as well.

Out of the corner of her eye Amelia caught sight of Matthew standing about half a block away looking for her.

"Oh, there's my friend," she said. "It was so nice to meet you."

Mike took her hand and said sincerely, "It was nice to meet you. Please come back next time you're around. I'm always here."

"I'll do that," said Amelia.

She turned to see if Matthew had seen her yet and she waved as he walked in her direction.

"I've gotta go." As she stood up Mike was still holding her hand like a lifeline.

"You will come back won't you?" he said urgently.

"If I'm ever here again. I promise. I will. 'Bye."

She walked toward Matthew and then turned to wave to Mike but he was gone and all at once she and Matthew were back in the cave.

Amelia hugged Matthew and said, "You'll never believe what happened to me!"

"Actually," he said, "I have a pretty good idea."

"You saw everything?" she asked, amazed.

"No. Not exactly that. Somehow I was able to 'feel' you. I couldn't see or hear anything, but I could sense . . . your feelings, your questions, the answers. Everything."

"How?"

He shrugged his shoulders and raised his eyebrows, "I don't know. It just happened. It's funny. I'm glad to see you, but in a way it's like we've never been apart."

"That's the first time I've been completely alone like that since we began this," she said. "I was a little nervous and scared but I never felt like I was *really* alone. It was more like I was, well, I don't know, being observed. Not the way a scientist observes rats in cages but more the way a mother would observe a child meeting a dog or cat for the first time." Amelia laughed. "That's funny. I never thought of it that way before."

"What do you mean?" asked Matthew.

"You know that voice I heard?"

Matthew nodded.

"Well, it said that I saw guilt where It saw innocence. And when I first found myself in the park and then talking to the man I was a little scared. But think about a two-year-old meeting a friendly St. Barnard for the first time: the child would probably be scared at first and then enjoy the dog. But the mother's not concerned. She knows nothing's going to harm the child. And that's how it felt . . . like I was being watched over and no harm could possibly come to me."

"Amelia," said Matthew, "Do you think that's a realistic way to look at things?"

"I don't know if it's realistic. It's just how I felt." She laughed. "And as Anna vould say, 'Everyt'ing ees bilief. Vhy not have entertainink biliefs?'"

Matthew laughed and gave Amelia a hug. "Come on, you! Let's go find Äsha and see what other adventures lie ahead."

They walked back to the mouth of the cave and discovered it was already dark. They stepped outside and were shocked to find themselves standing on the yard in front of the White House with Äsha. Suddenly they heard dogs barking viciously and turned to see five Dobermans pelting toward them.

"This way!" said Äsha as she disappeared right through the wall of the White House.

"Oh, my God!" screamed Amelia. "Has she forgotten that we don't know how to walk through walls?"

"Hey! Remember that *dog* analogy! Is *'mother'* aware that these are *not* friendly St. Barnards?" Matthew yelled, dancing in one spot since there was no place to run or hide.

"Äsha! Äsha!" yelled Amelia banging on the wall in a total panic.

Just then two of the dogs leapt into the air going for their throats. Matthew grabbed Amelia's hand and plunged "through" the wall dragging her with him. They lay on the floor gasping for breath. Matthew looked at Amelia and said, "Good thing impossibilities never occur! I *can't* believe Äsha did that to us!"

Suddenly Äsha appeared. "Did what?"

"You left us to be attacked by those dogs! How could you do that?"

"Those dogs wouldn't have touched you. Besides, you walked through the wall didn't you?"

Matthew and Amelia looked at each other as the realization hit that they had indeed walked, or more precisely hurtled, through a *wall!* Then Matthew thought about how scared they'd been.

"But still, Äsha," he said, "we could have been killed. And yes, I know there's no 'death' but that's hardly the point. We were really scared."

"Do you think you would have been afraid to try walking through a wall?" said Äsha. "You did see that it was possible with Timothy and still you didn't try."

"Oh, come on. That was different! You and Timothy always hang out in other dimensions. I'm sure you guys walk through walls and walk on water all the time!"

"So, were you afraid to try walking through walls?" asked Äsha.

"Of course I was afraid! That professor got pretty banged up on the boulders and *that* was just an illusion! This was a real wall!" argued Matthew.

"Based on results though, you put your fear aside and walked through the wall. Remember, it's *all illusion*," said Äsha.

"Those dogs wouldn't have felt like an illusion if they'd bitten us!" said Matthew still standing his ground.

"Those dogs," said Äsha, "are on a different dimension. They can see you, like the animals in India, but they can't touch you. You really were perfectly safe: just more motivated than usual."

Amelia and Matthew burst out laughing. Matthew had planned to stay angry until Äsha saw his point but it wasn't worth the effort.

"Come along," said Äsha. "It's time to go."

Matthew and Amelia jumped to their feet and hurriedly caught up with Äsha just as she walked through another wall.

Chapter XI

Walking Through Walls

They looked at each other and laughed. By this point, they were so exhausted from everything that had been happening, not to mention lack of food and sleep, they'd become punchy. Their analytical minds had finally given up the struggle and everything seemed hilariously funny.

Matthew stepped back a few paces and said, "Alright, 'Mother!' Hope you're watching!" He then pretended to be a vaudeville dancer and did a little dance routine moving sideways into the wall with his shoulder. There was a resounding thud but nothing happened.

Amelia giggled, and said, "Haven't you learned anything? That maneuver was just like that guy in India."

"Okay, Miss Amelia," said Matthew, folding his arms. "Let's see what you can do."

Amelia took a deep breath, stood with her back to the wall, closed her eyes and imagined the wall inside herself. From this vantage point, seeing the wall as a "wave," not a "particle," she just imagined herself being a part of the wall and the wall being a part of herself. Then she imagined moving through the wall to the other side and there she was!

She jumped in the air and clapped her hands. Then she stepped back through the wall and said, "*Viola!*"

Matthew laughed, "Isn't it *voilà*?"

"No," she said. "It's a wall! Come on!"

Amelia disappeared back through the wall. Matthew still couldn't figure it out. Suddenly, Amelia's arm appeared through the wall and her finger beckoned him. Matthew took her hand and found himself on the other side of the wall, too.

"You know, I don't know what's wrong with walking down the hall like a normal person," said Matthew as Amelia dragged him along. They were in what appeared to be a secret passageway. At the end of the hall stood Äsha in front of a door that looked like a huge vault. As soon as they saw her she disappeared through the door. When they reached the door Matthew said, "Amelia, this is one thick door! We're not talking a flimsy wall here!"

Amelia laughed, "Matthew, there's no difference."

"Oh, well. If there's no difference, why bother with a vault. They could just hang curtains!"

She said, "It's in your mind, silly!" Matthew sighed. "Stop trying to figure it out in your mind. It'll never work," said Amelia. "It's your fear that's stopping you. Think about . . . *loving* the door."

"Amelia, you are too much! 'Loving' a door? Now that's a first!"

"No, I really mean it!"

Matthew put on an "I'm-being-a-good-sport" face, walked up to the door, flung his arms out with his body pressed up against the vault door and said, "I love you, vault door!" Nothing happened. "See," he said from the same position.

Amelia stamped her foot, "Do you want to be '*right*' or do you want to get to the other side?"

"Can't I do both?" said Matthew, cracking a grin. "Oh, alright. I'll try again."

He leaned up against the door. At first he was only aware of the door being cold and hard but then he sensed that the door had an energy all it's own, the same as the fountain they'd seen earlier. With his eyes closed he could see the "color" of the door. It was a dark, steel grey. And then in his mind's eye he "saw" the door as molecules and finally atoms with huge empty spaces. As he continued "seeing" in this way he saw that the door was a wavy energy pattern with an electrical discharge here and there and a few dark spots. To be "seeing" this was a physicist's dream come true! Matthew felt so much joy and excitement from this vision that it was like being in love. He was about to tell Amelia what he was seeing but suddenly he found himself on the other side of the door with Amelia and Äsha standing next to him. Matthew would have said something but right in front of them were the President and two advisors. There were no windows and the room was totally sound proof.

"Sir," said a tall, thin man, addressing the President. "We've been aware of this problem for some time now but there's really no way to combat it."

"You see," said the other man, who was short and stocky, "because it's *mental* the cause of death appears to be natural. Even if we know who's doing it, we can't stop them, at least not in any legal way. And even if we were to have them killed quietly the fact is that they seem to know when we're coming. We can't even catch them."

The thin man said, "We feel certain they have some sort of a training camp here in this country but we can't find them through the normal channels and even if we do find them it would be like trying to storm Fort Knox."

"Well," said the President thoughtfully, "if they can attack us mentally, don't we have people who can attack back in the same way? And certainly someone should be able to find them. There seem to be plenty of psychics in the country these days."

"We've tried that," said the stocky man, "but these people are so well-trained they've created mental barriers we can't get through. And those that have gotten through with their minds have died sudden, violent deaths, right where they were sitting."

"The point we're trying to make, Sir," said the thin man, "is that there's no way to protect you. If these people want you dead, it will appear as a heart attack or a stroke but it will actually be these people killing you from the inside."

The President sighed, "Keep working on this. I'll get in touch with some people I know."

The men left the room and the President put his elbows on the desk with his head in his hands, sighed, and shook his head.

All at once, Amelia and Matthew found themselves back at the campground with Äsha. It was the middle of the night and the campground looked exactly as it did when Äsha had brought them back the first time.

Äsha said, "There was a yogi who once said, 'If you have nothing you can always sit on the side of the road and meditate.' Practice being quiet inside. Any question you have already has an answer. That answer is within yourself. You are a part of the unified field, the Universal Consciousness. Only your own belief can separate you from knowing everything you need to know. Simply ask. Then quietly listen. Now, lets look quickly at what you learned walking through walls and doors. What you both learned are basic, problem solving techniques that will work whether the wall is physical or mental. First you had to be **open** *to the possibility* that you could walk through a wall. Then you had to really want it; it had to be your **desire**, your **choice**." She stopped for a moment. "Are you both with me so far?"

Matthew and Amelia nodded.

"Then you had to **accept** that it was possible in order to **have it happen**. *You both had to visualize,* see the wall within, become a part of it and then *feel* what it would be like to move through it and be on the other side. Most important, you had to **Love** the wall . . . or anything that would appear to be an obstacle. There isn't a more powerful vibration in the universe than Love. But you must **feel Love** through your entire being. Love does not dominate or invade: it removes the blocks in consciousness by making you **one** with everyone and everything. Then simply *let go, let go, let go!* When you stop 'trying' and get your analytical mind out of the way, then things can happen! Oh, and don't forget to be *grateful* . . . opening your heart to say 'thank you' opens you up for all kinds of good things to happen. One more thing: whatever you say out loud has a vibration. Be sure that what you say is what you want in your life because it will be attracted to you!"

Right before their eyes Äsha began to disappear. Her body was becoming more and more transparent and her voice started sounding further and further away.

"Don't forget: Ask! Listen! Then *DO IT!*" Then at the very last moment she yelled, "In the morning everything will be the same and everything will be different!" And she totally vanished.

Chapter XII

The Abduction

Amelia whispered in exasperation, "That's it?! That's all she's going to tell us?! How can she do this to us?"

Matthew laughed and put his arm around her. "Amelia," he said while shaking his head, "stop trying so hard. Let's get some sleep." He gave her a big hug and kissed her. "See you in the morning."

She crawled into her tent and tried to make sense of everything. She wanted details! "Why can't I get straight answers from anyone?" she thought. She mulled everything over in her mind as she climbed into her sleeping bag. The next thing she knew it was morning. Everything was just as it had been. The instructor said exactly what she had said earlier except this time she looked at Amelia and said, "Amelia, you're on cleanup duty this morning."

Amelia had been trying to think of a sane explanation but now she was wondering whether she had subconsciously made up this whole adventure. At that moment Matthew's thought came to her as clearly as if he were speaking.

"Amelia, you did *not* make this up." Amelia quickly looked around to see if the other girls had noticed anything but they were getting dressed and chatting and no one seemed to notice a thing.

Amelia said silently, "Matthew, how did you know what I was thinking?"

"Well," said Matthew, "you're a loud thinker sometimes!"

Amelia burst out laughing and all the girls in the tent looked to see what was so funny. Amelia tried to muster a straight face and said, "Sorry. Private joke." With that, she sent a message to Matthew. "I'll meet you outside," she said.

They met just beyond the camp site where they could speak privately. Amelia said, "Now I know what Äsha meant when she said, 'Everything will be the same and everything will be different.' How could things ever be exactly the same again when you can hear another person thinking?"

Matthew laughed and said, "It's good to see you haven't lost your sense of humor!"

"Very funny, Matthew!" she said. "Now, seriously. What's the point of everything we've learned if we just come back here to the camp? What good can we do here?"

Matthew shook his head. "I don't know. We'll just have to wait and see."

Amelia had often been told that patience was not her long suit but before she could complain any further the instructor called all of the students together. "Alright, listen up everybody!" she yelled, clanking a pan with a spoon. After breakfast we'll be packing up and driving to Desolate Canyon. The good news: You'll have plenty of privacy. You'll be lucky if you see a hiker within 50 miles of the campground. The bad news: The reason there are no hikers is because there's no water. Since we'll have to take in our own water, water rationing is in, bathing is out!"

There was a combination moan-chuckle from the students and then the instructor said, "I expect to be on the road in one hour, so let's get a move on!"

Right on time the bus pulled out of the campground. Fortunately, nobody had enough energy to sing "99 Bottles of Beer on the Wall" the way they had on the trip down. They all sat quietly, either watching the scenery or taking cat naps. Apparently the combination of fresh air and lots of hiking had calmed even the most boisterous ones in the group. The bus slowly wound up and down dirt roads that had had little, if any, use since the end of the previous summer.

After two monotonous hours the bus clanked to a halt and sat forlornly in the dust, unwilling to move another inch. Everyone got out and gratefully stretched their legs. It quickly became apparent that this was a major problem not likely to be resolved in the near future.

Their instructor said, "Okay, kids. It looks like we're going to be here for awhile. We're going to have to wait until a car comes our way or until the county sheriff realizes we're missing. I registered our travel plans with the sheriff and in two days we're supposed to be checking out. When we don't show up they'll fly over our route to find us. It shouldn't be too difficult to locate a big yellow school bus so there's really nothing to worry about. We have plenty of food and water and we'll just pitch our tents right here.

"The only disadvantage is that we can't afford to split up in pairs this time. It would be too easy to get lost without trails and none of us are familiar with this area. We're all going to hike together in one group. So, let's set up camp, have lunch, and then we'll go for a hike and see what we can find."

Nobody was particularly pleased about having to hike in this area. It was hot, flat and barren of everything except the hardiest desert plants. However, it was the only viable option and it certainly beat sitting around in a bus for two days.

After lunch everyone set out for a hike, including the bus driver who had nothing better to do. Everything was quite flat except for some outcroppings that were about three miles away, so they headed toward them. In less than an hour they reached the outcroppings which turned out to be about 500 feet high. The group split up to look for rock samples but after only five minutes one of the students yelled, "Hey, everybody! Over here! Hurry!"

Everyone scrambled over rocks and gasped when they saw a hidden entrance leading to a manmade cave. The amazing part was that the entrance was tall enough for a semi and wide enough for two trucks to pass easily, yet it would have been impossible to see the entrance from the air because of the rock configurations concealing it. Before the instructor had a chance to object, most of the students had already begun exploring the cave. It seemed to be some kind of a deserted military outpost. The instructor yelled after them, "Alright. You may look around but stay TOGETHER!"

The cave entrance sloped gradually downward for about one hundred yards, until it finally leveled out and opened up into a huge cavern that also had been man-made. Even with twenty flashlights they seemed engulfed in darkness. A ledge had been carved into the rock about twenty feet above their heads. Some kids wanted to climb up and take a look but the instructor got there and nixed the idea.

From the other end of the cavern someone yelled, "Look! This boulder is actually an entranceway!" Everyone gathered around with their flashlights. It was easy to see that the boulder had been cut to look like part of the wall. However, no one could figure out how it operated.

Everyone looked around for a clue as to how the door worked but all they discovered were dusty tracks. It was impossible to tell how fresh the tracks were, partially because they had all been tromping around, but also because the cave would have changed very little even after years and years of desertion. Finally, everyone was getting bored. There was obviously no way for them to get in and the trail was just a dead end.

The instructor said, "Everybody! Gather 'round, please." They all assembled around the instructor. "It looks like this is the end of our excitement for today. Now, before it gets too late, let's go outside and see if we can't get a few rock samples before we head back to camp."

Children of Light

There were a few grumbles from those who were determined to get beyond the boulder but, in general, most everyone was looking forward to being outside again. They all began moving through the cavern toward the tunnel when suddenly huge spotlights, hidden from their view on the ledges above, blazed in their faces. They all froze in their tracks like animals blinded by headlights on a dark country road.

A man's voice blasted over of an audio system and echoed in the cavern, "You will all stay where you are. If anyone attempts to leave this cave you will be shot. Follow our instructions and you will not be hurt." With that, the boulder swung slowly inward. The voice commanded, "You will all step inside."

Everyone moved through the entrance into a brightly lit hall where they were ordered to line up in single file. Several guards in dark blue uniforms stood silently with automatic weapons pointed at them. Amelia watched the door swing back into place. Only the front of it was made to look like rock. The rest of it was more like a gigantic door on a bank vault, only large enough to accommodate a truck the size of a semi. The door was about three or four feet thick. When it banged shut, thick steel bolts slid automatically into place.

A sturdy looking man with dark hair and a scar on his cheek moved purposefully toward them. He commanded, "Face the wall." He then walked down the line of students and stared at each one intently.

Matthew and Amelia had been separated in the shuffle and when the man was very close to Matthew Amelia sent him a silent message.

The Abduction

"Matthew, clear your mind. Don't let on what you know!"

At that moment the man's head jerked around and he looked directly at Amelia as if she had spoken out loud. He walked right up to her, motioned to a guard and said, "Take this girl to a private cell. I don't want her to see any of the other prisoners." Immediately Amelia was taken down the hall and onto an elevator.

The instructor quickly said, "Excuse me sir, but I think there's been a terrible mistake here. These are just high school students . . ."

"SILENCE!" yelled the man. "I warn you. If anyone attempts to talk, I guarantee they will be shot." The man then resumed walking down the line from student to student. When he reached Matthew he stopped. His eyes narrowed and a wicked smile curled on the edge of his lips.

"So, you're Matthew." He then walked quickly down the rest of the line and said, "I want these prisoners taken to cell block 'A.'" He then pointed to Matthew and said, "Confine this one separately."

Immediately the group was led down a series of corridors to a large freight elevator. They descended fifteen levels before the elevator ground to a halt. It was quite warm and stuffy as they were led down the hall and through another vault-like door which automatically closed and locked behind them.

When they reached the cell block the teacher and bus driver were put into one cell and the students were all separated into small groups of three or four. Matthew was placed in a cell alone.

The cells were tiny and had nothing in them except a bare light bulb hanging from a two-story ceiling. After they had all been locked into their cells the guards went back through the door, locked it, and turned off the lights. Apparently the rooms were soundproof because Matthew couldn't hear anything except his own breathing.

Then he heard, "Matthew."

"Amelia, where are you? Are you alright?" he said in his mind.

"I'm fine," she replied. "I'm not sure where I am, but this place is immense. We went past some kind of a room full of power generators. I think they generate electricity for the entire building but I couldn't really tell. Also, I'm quite sure these people are doing experiments with telepathy or some kind of mind control. I can really feel their thoughts in certain parts of the building. There's a horrible feeling of death here; a lot of frightened people. Have you discovered anything?"

"No, not really," he replied, "but I'm almost sure the guards know nothing. I can easily reach their thoughts. I can even control them a bit. I made the guard think he had locked my cell when he didn't. But I still can't go anywhere because I don't know the combination to the door at the end of the hall."

"Matthew, there's something else I need to tell you," said Amelia. "I overheard that man with the scar on his face. Well, actually, I sort of listened in, but he said that you and I would make interesting 'specimens.' We've got to get out of here!"

Matthew said, "I can't do anything unless that door's opened. Until then we'd better stop talking, just to be on the safe side. I love you, Amelia."

Amelia smiled to herself and despite the cold she felt warm all over. In the dark she felt her way along the wall over to the door. She banged on the heavy door and tried to open it but it was locked tight. Amelia sank to the floor and began to cry.

She was totally alone and escape seemed impossible. Even if Matthew got out of his cell, how would he find her? And if they could escape, how would they get past the automatic bolting system on the main door, not to mention miles and miles of desert with no place to hide? Amelia felt more alone than she'd ever been in her life.

Matthew sat on the floor of his cell trying to think about Äsha. What was it that she really wanted them to understand? Ideas like 'things are thoughts' didn't do them any good now that they were back to real life. He couldn't walk through doors anymore nor could he just simply disappear from his cell and reappear in safety. His ability to communicate with Amelia wasn't much comfort since there was nothing he could do to help her. Suddenly the lights came on. Matthew jumped up and tried to figure out what was happening. A guard opened the window on his cell door and peered in. Matthew decided to do some experimenting.

Children of Light

He directed his thought toward the guard, "This is the wrong cell." The guard yelled, "Get one from the next cell." He then turned to close the window. Matthew closed his eyes and thought, "You don't need to close that window." The guard turned and walked away, leaving the window open. Matthew walked carefully up to the window and watched them pull Tom Jenkens out of the next cell.

Tom was a small kid with red hair and freckles. Matthew had hiked with him the summer before. He was an excellent geology student but a poor hiking partner since he was petrified of heights. Tom looked like a little mouse compared to the huge guards. When they reached the door Matthew concentrated on the guard using the combination. The guard opened a box in the wall and punched in a code. As if someone had spoken to him, Matthew heard the code. "158A 239C 115C."

Though he was sure this was the code, he was taking no chances. Just as the lights were turned off he quietly slid out of his unlocked cell, closed it, and squeezed through the main door just before it slammed shut. Fortunately, there were very few people in this area of the building and everything was extremely well marked with partial floor plans on each level just outside the elevator. Matthew watched as the elevator went up five flights and stopped. It didn't move again so he assumed that was where they had taken Tom. He couldn't risk the elevator so he took the emergency stairs.

On his way up he psychically contacted Amelia. "Amelia, I'm out of my cell. Are you still alright?"

She said, "I'm fine. A little cold, but I'm fine."

The Abduction

"Listen," said Matthew, "they've taken Tom and I'm following them. Hopefully, I'll be able to figure out what's going on here. I can't tell you more just yet except for the fact that the guards are very weak minded. If you get into trouble try to reach their thoughts."

Matthew cautiously emerged but there wasn't a clue as to which direction they had taken Tom. He moved quickly down one of the corridors and then stopped abruptly when he heard voices in a room. There were about fifty men in the room, their ages ranging from about eighteen to thirty-five. They were dressed in regular civilian clothes and apparently had assembled for a lecture.

Matthew heard guards coming toward him down the hall. He figured it would be better to join the class than to be spotted standing around in the hall, so he slid into a seat at the back of the class. A moment later the door closed and the lecture began.

A tall, thin man with blue eyes and blondish-grey hair stepped up to the podium. Behind him was a floor-to-ceiling curtain that stretched the width of the room. He said, "Gentlemen, over the past weeks we have discussed the power of the human mind. Today you will witness it's weaknesses."

He flicked a switch on the podium and the curtain behind him automatically drew back while the lights dimmed.

He continued, "As you can see, we are behind a two-way mirror. The man you see blindfolded and tied in the chair is thirty-five years old and is in perfect health. He has been told that his arm has been cut and that he is going to be allowed to bleed to death. As you can all see, there is nothing trickling down his arm except water which has been warmed to body temperature. Please observe a man bleeding to death without ever losing a drop of blood."

Matthew watched in horror as the man first fought to get free and then slowly gave up the fight. Soon his head began to wobble and in a fairly short amount of time the struggle was over. His head flopped down to his chest.

The speaker pushed a button on the podium and said, "Is there a pulse?"

A man in the next room shook his head and said, "No, sir. He's dead."

"Good," said the instructor. "Please prepare for the next experiment."

With that, the curtains closed, the lights were turned on, and the man continued with his speech.

"You have all just witnessed the effects of the human mind over the body. That man believed that blood kept him alive and that a lack of blood would kill him. But, since he clearly lost no blood, it was obviously his mind that killed him.

"Now gentlemen, this is what we're looking for. We want the human mind to do our work for us. You will never see a coroner's report that says 'Cause of death: Mind killing the body.' When we do our work properly, the report will either say 'Cause of death unknown' or 'due to natural causes'.

The Abduction

"We've done much experimentation in hospitals. We've told patients they were in a bed where someone had recently died of a highly contagious disease. Although the story was a total fabrication, most of the patients unfailingly developed the same disease and died. We found that the few who did not become ill generally knew little about the disease and had a strong will to live whereas those who died were very familiar with and frightened by the disease.

"Fear kills, and we have refined this process greatly. Now I will show you an experiment in which the victim will not be told anything on a conscious level. Instead he will be hypnotized."

Matthew could barely fathom the way this man so casually talked about murdering people. But there was also something peculiar about his speech pattern. It was too perfect for him to have spoken English as a native language, yet there was no clue as to nationality. When he thought about it, everyone seemed to speak that way yet no one ever spoke in another language.

Again the curtains drew back as the lights dimmed. There stood Tom, blindfolded on a chair. He had already been hypnotized and a man in the room was telling Tom that he was standing on the edge of a precipice. Tom stood there shaking and trembling.

"Please, sir. Please let me get away from the edge."

"No, Tom," said the man. "Either you jump off the edge or you will be pushed."

Tears streamed down Tom's face, "Please, don't make me do this. I'll . . . I'll die if you make me jump."

"That's right, Tom," replied the man. "You are going to die."

Matthew closed his eyes and started trying to contact Tom. It was extremely difficult because Tom was deeply under hypnosis. Matthew felt as if he were trying to race through hip-deep mud in order to reach Tom before it was too late. He persisted and finally he reached him.

In his mind he said, "Tom. Listen to me. It's Matthew."

Tom's head jerked up and he said out loud, "Matthew! Matthew! Please tell them not to do this to me! Please! I don't want to die!"

Matthew continued, "Tom, you're *not* on the edge of a precipice. You are being made to believe it's true but it's not. You're standing on a chair."

Tom began to relax and the instructor bellowed, "Who's interfering with this experiment!"

The lights came on and everyone looked around. All eyes focused on Matthew. "So, Matthew, you think you can outsmart me with your infantile mind games. Watch very carefully."

Four guards surrounded Matthew and held him while the man stepped off the podium and walked through a door into the room beyond. Matthew tried desperately to reach Tom's thought but there was no

The Abduction

response. It was as if Tom were surrounded by an impenetrable wall.

The man walked over to Tom and said coldly, "I'm sorry you didn't jump on your own. That would have been easier. I'm afraid I'll have to push you."

Tom screamed as the man pushed him off the chair. He fell to the floor with a hard thud and lay there motionless. A medic checked Tom's pulse and said, "He's dead."

The blonde man turned and faced Matthew, who was still standing at the back of the classroom.

He said, "Cause of death?"

The man said, "It appears to be a heart attack, sir."

"Guards," said the blonde man. "Bring Matthew in here."

Matthew walked into the room as Tom's motionless body was removed on a stretcher. The room was cleared and the man said, "Matthew, we're all so grateful that you could volunteer for our program. We've been needing more of a challenge and it appears that you are going to provide it."

Chapter XIII

Instruments of Hate

Everyone cleared out of the room and Matthew was left with nothing but a chair. Suddenly, he felt all the oxygen being sucked out of the air. Matthew found himself gasping for breath. Dizzy, he dropped to his hands and knees.

"Amelia!" he said in his mind. "They're trying to kill me! Somehow they're taking all of the oxygen out of the room."

"Matthew!" said Amelia right away. "They've hypnotized you!"

"No one's here!" said Matthew.

"Matthew! Stop it! Listen to me! It's an illusion!"

"Are you sure?"

"I can see everything from here," she said. "There's a man behind a glass window. In his mind he's 'throwing' pictures at you. He's imaging you suffocating."

"What can I do?" Matthew asked, barely able to breathe.

Amelia searched for an answer, then said, "Remember the man in India, how we helped him? We'll do the same thing for you. Just see yourself the same way."

Amelia closed her eyes and saw Matthew with a beautiful golden light shining on him and penetrating through the crown of his head into the rest of his body. Then the light radiated out from his body and she saw him peaceful, breathing freely.

Matthew immediately relaxed and began taking slow, deep breaths.

"It's working, Amelia!"

The door flung open and slammed against the wall. The man said angrily, "I want that girl here. Now!"

"Amelia! They're coming for you. Get out if you can!"

Amelia knew the man wanted her dead. She could feel his intentions. She knew she wasn't strong enough to take him on by herself; escape was her only chance for survival. She was sitting in the middle of an empty room in pitch darkness, so she crawled in the direction of the door and felt her way along the wall until she reached the handle. Then she gave the door a good hard shove. It was quite solid. She thought, "This is impossible. I'm not in some other dimension! I can't do those things anymore!"

She was angry, confused and genuinely frightened. Everything she'd just learned swirled in her mind. Even if she could remember anything helpful there wasn't enough time. Words drifted through her mind. "There is no time. There is no death. There is no matter." Those ideas made her even angrier.

"What good is it?!" she yelled out loud angrily. "I want to live *here*, not in some other dimension!"

The room seemed darker and colder and Amelia felt miserably alone and lost. She had no idea what she should do. Then she remembered Äsha saying "Ask" and, since there was nothing else she could do, she sank to the floor with her back up against the wall and said aloud, "What do I need to know?"

She sat quietly and, though she didn't hear literal words, the message she received was "Open your heart." She saw the image she'd seen of Time, where it looked like a three dimensional chess board in which the past, present, and future were all one. Then she was shown that it was essentially the same with the different dimensions.

The dimensions were "layered waves." They weren't separate; they were all one. In the same way that she learned about subatomic waves and particles being one, and that the wave became a particle through observation, she saw that the dimensions would shift from being 'waves' into 'particles,' from *possibility* to *reality*, according to what she was choosing to see or believe.

Amelia realized she was a part of all dimensions but it was where she chose to *focus* that caused that dimension to become "solid," to become reality. If she focused on herself in the third dimension then along with it came all the physical laws and limitations, because part of being in the third dimension is the *belief* that everything is outside, objective. She could see that if she focused on a different dimension that her *choice* to *see* that dimension made it reality.

She remembered how she felt when she was inside the White House. She'd been too tired and giddy to analyze the situation and in her laughter she'd abandoned rational thought. It was like being intoxicated and telling everyone you love them. Only Amelia had felt in love with everything around her, including the wall.

Amelia smiled as these feelings re-occurred for her and suddenly she found herself sitting in the hall outside her cell. Amelia jumped to her feet and said enthusiastically, "Oh, thank you, thank you, thank you!"

She mentally sent a message to Matthew saying she was alright and had escaped but that she wouldn't communicate further for both their sakes.

Her first thought was to search for Matthew but right away she sensed there was something else she needed to do first. Initially Amelia had planned to take a passage that she felt sure would lead to Matthew but now she was impelled to go in the opposite direction. She walked through a maze of corridors and then found herself standing in front of two huge doors painted bright orange with some kind of strange symbol in black. Though the doors were securely locked and bolted, Amelia knew she was to go inside.

This time she walked through the doors without hesitation. Inside, the halls were deserted. Amelia walked down the long corridor and again she felt guided to a particular area. She couldn't see a door so she simply walked through the wall and found herself in a laboratory filled with hundreds of small animals.

There were mainly wild animals plus some cats and dogs and they'd all been marked with some kind of green dye. The room had a foul stench and all of the animals were crowded into tiny, filthy cages that didn't even leave them enough room to turn around. There was no food or water in any of the cages and most of the animals looked like they were dying. Many had infected, open wounds and eyes that were swollen shut. In one corner of the room was a pile of mostly dead animals. Some were just barely alive and trying to crawl out from under the others. Amelia collapsed on the floor in tears. She was angry and sickened by the horrible display of cruelty.

Helplessness blanketed her and she was engulfed in total darkness. Until that moment she hadn't realized she was seeing without the aid of any material form of light. She was literally blind with anger. She lay in shock, crying uncontrollably, her whole body shaking on the floor.

"I can't do this," she thought. "Why did anyone think I could make a difference here?"

She knew the energy that allowed her to walk through walls and see in the dark was gone and now she was locked in with no apparent way out. Then she remembered the advisors warning the President of people who could kill using their minds. These had to be the people they were talking about!

She realized that Äsha must have known this was going to happen. "But why would Matthew and I be chosen?" she thought. "We're only in high school. We're not trained to deal with mental assassins. What were they thinking sending us here?" And then Amelia struggled with who "they" were.

After a while she sat up and a moment later she felt a small animal climb up into her lap. She petted it and discovered it was a baby rabbit. "Oh, you poor thing," she said as she gently scooped it up and held it to her heart.

Then she remembered the words she heard in the park, "You see the innocence of these little ones, that the scars were put there by someone else. Recognize this in all your brothers and sisters, too."

Amelia wondered how she could find innocence in these people. She thought, "These people aren't innocent and they don't deserve to be forgiven!"

For the first time she thought about Tom. She'd felt everything Matthew had gone through to save him and she shared his feelings when Tom died. Amelia had never known such cruelty really existed and she began to wonder if any of them would survive.

Suddenly, in a vision, Amelia saw herself during a thunder storm, tied up and floating on the ocean in a coffin. Blinding rain pelted her face and skin. The coffin rocked wildly from the wind and waves beating against the sides. Then she saw floating above her the faces of the men involved with killing Tom and experimenting on the animals. Amelia felt raw, blind rage and in her anger everything she saw turned a murky red.

She tried to yell but no one heard her over the storm. Though she couldn't move, she could see that lashed onto her hand was a hammer with the word "Hate" written in blood. Her feelings of anger began to create steel-plated armor around her body. She saw the word "Resentment" and felt armor clamp onto her right leg; "Rage" clamped onto the left leg; "Revenge" was the breastplate; "Fear" was the back. Finally, a heavy helmet with a visor snapped into place and said "Victim."

She could see all her classmates and teachers from the field trip in the visor of the helmet. They were standing on a cliff high above where she was floating in the water. Below them the ocean crashed against huge boulders. To Amelia's horror, she watched as they were pushed one by one from the cliff, dying instantly when they hit the rocks below. Then she saw a bulldozer dump all the animals from the lab over the edge also. When she looked through the visor she could still see the faces floating above her. Only this time she could see their upper bodies, too. She noticed they were each grasping a hammer identical to the one in her hand with "Hate" written in blood. They coldly stared back at her, somehow making her responsible for every death.

"I'm not responsible!" she screamed. "I didn't do all this! I'm not these people!" Amelia wept. Hot tears dripped onto the little rabbit in her lap making its fur damp. "I'm just a kid!" she cried. "What can I do?"

The vision continued. She lay trapped in the coffin. The lid slammed shut and with each feeling of fear or helplessness a nail was pounded into the coffin by the ones floating above her. As this happened her fear changed to panic and anguish. Finally, the coffin began to sink. Amelia felt water washing up around her body as the coffin tilted to one side and was sucked into the ocean.

She felt herself utterly give up as she plummeted down through murky, green seaweed. The coffin hit bottom with a dull thud and began rocking in the undercurrent. Amelia waited to die but instead she was surrounded by stillness.

She'd never known this kind of silence nor the peace that followed. She was no longer in any pain. The coffin fell apart as the armor and ropes detached. Amelia found herself swimming, naked, breathing under water. As she swam she heard whales and dolphins singing and she realized she understood their songs! Not in her mind but in her heart.

They were singing about life as peaceful and joyous, filled with love and eternal light. They sang songs about being from the stars and then Amelia saw something she'd never recognized before. The whales and dolphins were dancing! She could feel their feelings and it was exactly the way she felt the night she danced with Matthew.

What a contrast from the surface where storms tore the sky, whipping the waves to a frenzy as they crashed against the rocks and beat upon the shore. But in the depths of the ocean all was calm, untouched by surface events.

Then Amelia saw everyone who'd been pushed from the cliff, including the animals, swimming and "dancing." Her friends all smiled and waved at her. Amelia's body jerked. The vision ended. She found herself still sitting in the dark with the baby rabbit on her lap.

She wasn't totally sure what the vision meant but she was much calmer and could finally think more clearly. From her mother Amelia had learned a little bit about dream interpretation. She'd write down her dream and after each line she'd skip a line. With a different colored pen she'd write down her feelings about whatever was on the line above. Then an entirely different dream would emerge based on subconscious feelings. Since she didn't have a pen and paper, or light for that matter, Amelia decided to just go over it in her mind bit by bit to see if there was a clue that might help.

The beginning of the vision was easy to understand. Her mother taught her that water represented emotion and she could see her feelings reflected both in the storm and the turbulent ocean. She could see her feelings of being trapped easily enough but she couldn't quite understand the faces floating above the coffin. Then she remembered her mother saying that sometimes dream images are figurative.

"Of course!" thought Amelia, "Faces! What is it I don't want to face?"

She remembered how all the faces turned red when she was angry and thought, "I can't face my anger. I can't face all the anger I feel. I'm no different from them. I'd feel no compassion, no regret or remorse if they died." Amelia was a bit shocked by this realization. She'd always thought of herself as a loving person incapable of hating or harming another.

Instruments of Hate

The only difference between her hatred and theirs was that Amelia felt she had a right to be angry. Then she remembered a teacher in her drama class who said, "If you're playing the role of a 'bad guy' and you think you're bad, you'll never be believable! Even the worst ax-murderer *thinks* he's right -- in the moment! He may decide a moment later that it was a horrible thing to do and kill himself, but at the time he felt justified."

She thought about the hammer with the word "Hate" written in blood and it reminded her of something she'd heard earlier. Anna had said that a hammer wasn't inherently "good or bad;" it was an instrument. Suddenly the meaning clicked. It didn't matter what her reasons were for hating or the reasons the men had for hating; all of them, herself included, were "instruments" of hate. Anna had said that the "instrument" wasn't inherently good or bad.

"That's where innocence is!" Amelia yelled out loud. She realized that the consciousness she recognized as her own, the unified field, Universal Consciousness, included these men. They all shared the same essential nature, the same consciousness.

At first it was an unbelievable concept but then she thought, "If someone were to see me right now as my emotions, they'd think I was a horribly angry and hateful person. But I know that's not me. So, what if everything I see in these men isn't who they really are either?"

She then made the connection with the "children" who emerged from the man and woman in the park. She realized that the children's idea of love was a distortion;

it was a mistake but it was a mistake they'd *learned*. The mistake wasn't who they were; the distortion wasn't their nature.

Amelia thought, "What if my feelings are a mistake?" She began to think about hatred as a distortion of love. If she didn't love Tom and small animals then she'd have no reason to hate the men for cruelty and murder. She realized she'd managed to twist love into hate; she had used love as a reason to hate. And even though she didn't know what motivated these men she began to feel that somehow they'd done the same thing; their idea of love must also have been distorted.

The vision came back into Amelia's mind. She saw the armor with all the words. She could see that she was literally trapped by her own anger. She was a bit confused by the meaning of the helmet with the word "Victim." She tried to think of what a helmet would symbolize. "Protection," she thought. "But then how does victim connect with protection; what does the visor mean?"

Then Amelia realized it was also a way of not being seen. No one could see her face. She thought back to her earlier realization about not being able to face her own hatred. Being a "victim" was her visor. It was literally a mask to keep people from seeing what she couldn't face: her own deplorable feelings of anger and hatred.

She thought about how the "faces" had made her feel responsible for the animals and people being killed and how she yelled, "I'm not responsible!" Then she thought of Äsha saying, "Do you have the ability to respond positively?"

All at once she saw the big picture. Being a victim shielded her from any responsibility for her own feelings. "I've been thinking I'm not responsible. I can't respond positively because I'm a victim."

Clearly the "nails" in the coffin were representing her own negative emotions literally "sealing" her fate, but her feelings were so different when she finally sank below the surface. She thought, "If water is emotion, then what are the symbols I'm seeing in this vision?" The words "surface appearance" drifted through Amelia's mind and then Äsha's words "Fear: False Evidence Appearing Real."

The common denominator of everything she'd felt on the "surface" was fear but it was just an appearance. Underneath, it was peaceful, calm; Amelia felt loved. It was an entirely different reality. Like a puzzle she began piecing it all together in her mind. From an emotional point of view the ocean represented the Universal Consciousness of Love. On the surface was fear -- a distortion of love, not the reality.

All of a sudden she saw the choice she'd been making. She'd been trapped on the surface by her own fear. Thoughts were like the "waves" Timothy had talked about. When she focused on the surface thoughts of fear, then fear became real even as the waves became particles through observation. When she focused below the surface, on what was peaceful, calm and unchanging, then that was her reality.

Children of Light

She thought of how she felt swimming naked, breathing under water, hearing the whales and dolphins singing, and being a part of that incredible dance; what it was like to see her friends and the little animals in the ocean alive and well as if they had simply gone home.

Amelia's analytical mind stepped in: "The Critic," as her mother would say. The conversation went like this: "Amelia, dear. That's all very well and good, but let's be realistic. Thinking 'nicely' about wicked people or believing that you all come from some big ocean of love is not going to save you or anyone else. Get a grip!"

Amelia knew better than to argue with The Critic so she did what her mother taught her and said, "Thank you for sharing." She then prepared her defense and said, "To tell you the truth, I don't know whether I'm right. I may have reasoned this out incorrectly. However, believing that we all come from an 'ocean of love' and that we never die is making me happy. And at this particular moment in time I'd rather be happy than right."

She thought to herself, "That was pretty good!" as she petted the bunny in her lap. In the dark she smiled thinking of the animals as she'd seen them in the vision. They were all healthy and alive and they were at home in this ocean of love.

Gradually the room got lighter. Amelia looked around and, using a hose she found in a sink, filled every available container with water. She opened the cages and the animals all rushed to the water and drank. With perfect ease she walked back through the wall, down the corridor and through the orange doors.

Instruments of Hate

Again Amelia was compelled to walk through a series of corridors and down several flights of stairs. It seemed that she was in a portion of the building that was rarely used because she never saw anyone. Finally, she was led to a doorway that was invisible from where she stood. Amelia walked through the door and found herself in a round room hand-carved out of the rock.

In the center was a spiral staircase winding down several flights. On the walls torches burned in iron holders that were molded to look like strange and wicked creatures. The walls and ceiling were blackened from smoke and there was the stench of dead animals and burning hair combined with putrid odors Amelia could not identify. Her first instinct was to turn and run but she knew she was there for a purpose. Still she was gripped with terror as she walked down the rock stairway. Shadows flickered in eerie formations across the walls.

She tried to overcome her fear but nothing seemed to work. Then Amelia remembered her grandmother teaching her the 91st Psalm when she was a child. Her grandmother said, "This is a Psalm of great protection. You must memorize it." Amelia had memorized it but she was only ten years old at the time and now she could only remember bits and pieces of it. She said quietly to herself, "He that dwelleth in the secret place of the Most High shall abide under the shadow of the Almighty."

As she stepped down, two rats squealed and ran down the steps in front of her. Amelia's heart pounded as she clung to the railing for support. She breathed deeply and looked carefully at the next step before continuing. "Thou shalt not be afraid of the terror by night; nor for the pestilence that walketh in darkness." Amelia's mind went blank. "Why didn't I do a better job of memorizing this?" she thought. "Of course, I don't think that even Grandma would have imagined this place." She then stepped over a dead something-or-other without stopping to see what it was and said, "His truth shall be thy shield and buckler." Amelia couldn't remember any more but, fortunately, she'd made it to the bottom of the stairs by that time.

She walked into a cavernous area. The ceiling was about thirty feet high and in front of her was some kind of entrance with a huge round slab of rock in front of it. The rock was perfectly flat, about fifteen feet in diameter and ten inches thick. Apparently it rolled on a track but Amelia had no idea how this could be accomplished.

On either side of the entrance were burning torches set in holders with wickedly smiling faces that were half human and half animal. Though everything inside her was telling Amelia to go back, she walked directly toward the stone and it seemed to just disappear as she walked through it.

On the other side she found herself in some kind of a bizarre religious temple. It was immense, with a ceiling so high that even with torches on all the walls it was enveloped in darkness. There were benches carved out of stone that would seat at least a thousand people. Hanging along the wall close to the entrance were black, hooded cloaks. On the walls were symbols that Amelia had never seen before. One was a five-pointed star with a goat's head in the middle and another was an upside-down pyramid with an eye in the center.

Instruments of Hate

As Amelia got closer she realized the symbols had been painted in blood and outlined with melted gold. There were crude African masks and relief carvings depicting the most horrible acts of violence and cruelty imaginable. Smiling skeletons, snakes, gargoyles, and other creatures, all with vicious faces and molded out of gold, silver and copper, watched Amelia as she walked down the aisle. Shadows danced across the room as she moved slowly and cautiously down to the blood-stained altar.

On the altar she found a human skull in the center. Behind it were seven black candles in a V-shaped candelabra. Arranged around it were a mortar and pestle, a chalice, copper trays, a whip, a long, braided leather rope, and a huge crystal on top of a mirror. In front of the altar on the floor were two circles made with shiny black pebbles, one inside the other. The diameter of the larger circle was about five feet and the circle inside was about three feet. In the center was a five-sided star and in the space between the two circles was an inscription in Latin. About ten feet behind the altar, raised on a black marble platform, was a four foot long salamander made out of gold with ruby eyes. Surrounding the salamander and beneath it were small holes in the marble which produced flames that rose all around it. A few feet behind the salamander was a large black curtain about twenty feet high.

It was made of a heavy, coarse material and was emblazoned with an upside-down crucifix entwined with golden snakes. Amelia knew that she had to go behind the curtain and this was at least part of the reason she had been brought here, but she thought, "Oh, please. I don't want to know what's back there."

Then, almost as if someone had spoken to her, she heard "Amelia, you have the strength. You're of the Light; darkness cannot touch you."

Amelia stepped behind the curtain and followed a stone staircase down to a concealed chamber. She walked through the locked door and before her were rows and rows of glass jars neatly lettered and in alphabetical order.

There were various herbs and extracts. Some were common, like marjoram, cinnamon, or salt, while others Amelia had never heard of. There was also a huge ceramic jar labeled "Opium." Hanging on the wall behind it Amelia recognized censers that were usually used for burning incense in Catholic masses. On one wall there were hundreds of very old books which dealt with everything from black, satanic ritual and voodoo to conjuring up spirits, casting spells and making poisons.

Next to the books were shelves with jars containing different animals preserved in some kind of liquid. There were lizards, snakes, bats, toads, frogs, a host of other small animals and various internal organs.

She heard something scurrying across the floor, turned quickly, and nearly knocked a glass jar off the ledge behind her. Somehow she managed to grab it and then she nearly dropped it when she saw it contained a human hand. Trembling, Amelia replaced the jar on the ledge and turned to leave, but there was one room she still hadn't seen.

Instruments of Hate

She forced herself to walk to the open doorway. A strong, putrid odor rose up to meet her as she descended a few more steps into the room. There she saw the charred bones of children and infants who had obviously been used as human sacrifices. Amelia grabbed the wall as unconsciousness swept over her.

The next thing she knew, she was hearing a loud grating noise from above. Using the doorway she pulled herself up to a standing position and walked unsteadily up the steps, past the glass jars, and up the stairway. She looked cautiously out from behind the curtain and saw that the huge stone was being rolled away from the entrance.

Amelia knew her only chance of remaining unrecognized was to get a hold of one of the hooded cloaks next to the entrance. She could hear chanting outside of the door as the rock slowly moved aside and she ran faster than she thought she could up the aisle. She grabbed a cloak, threw it on, and then squashed herself up against the wall in the midst of the cloaks.

Amelia was afraid she'd be discovered immediately but no one even looked in her direction. The first one to enter the room was a man whose face and head were invisible beneath the head of a mountain goat. Between the ram's three-foot horns was a black candle. The man was wearing a black robe embroidered with snakes and other satanic emblems.

Following him were four girls that Amelia knew. They were dressed in black, almost sheer material embroidered with the same emblems the high priest had on his robe. They wore necklaces made of gold. The first girl wore a snake with emerald eyes. The girl following her had a necklace made of two salamanders linked at the tail with their heads meeting to form a 'V'. Both salamanders had ruby eyes like the one behind the altar.

The third girl had a necklace that had a man's body with the legs and head of a goat and huge wings on his back. Between the horns of the goat was a torch and the flame was represented by a huge diamond. The last girl had a necklace with the sun, the moon and the planets. Small diamonds, emeralds and rubies represented stars and dangled from a golden collar by gold threads. Amelia realized immediately they'd all been hypnotized.

The girls walked slowly down the aisle carrying black velvet pillows. The first pillow had an ebony handled dagger; the second, a sword; the third, a wand; and the fourth had a five-pointed star. Behind them were four boys Amelia recognized from the field trip. They too had been hypnotized. The boys walked stiffly and looked straight ahead as they swung censers which burned something with a pungent odor. She tried to reach their thoughts but it was like trying to see through a heavy cloud.

Behind the boys were hundreds of men, all dressed in animal costumes. They howled, grunted and snuffled as they moved slowly into the room. The men at the front moved unsteadily as if they were drugged and then Amelia realized that they were probably burning opium in the censers. From the pictures on the walls Amelia had a good idea of what was about to happen but she didn't know how to help.

Instruments of Hate

A man dressed as a crow walked away from the crowd and headed directly toward Amelia. She tried to disappear into the cloaks but he had obviously spotted her.

A familiar voice whispered, "Amelia, don't be afraid. It's me. This way." With her head down and her hood pulled as far forward as possible Amelia walked closely behind Matthew. They sat by themselves on a bench just behind the rest of the group. Through telepathy they began to talk.

Amelia said, "Matthew I can't tell you everything I've seen, but we're all in unbelievable danger."

Matthew quietly took Amelia's hand and said, "I know everything you've been through and I know exactly what you've seen. I was in my cell when the guards selected four boys and four girls and took them from their cells. I wasn't sure what was happening until you came into this temple.

"I saw you walk through walls and then I realized I could do the same thing. I followed the guards to the room where everybody dressed and as they all left I slipped into one of the rooms, grabbed this costume, and joined the crowd."

"Matthew, why didn't you talk to me until now?"

"Because I have this feeling someone's been listening to us. I can't explain it, but I was afraid that if I spoke to you I'd put you in danger. Even now it's risky."

Amelia nodded her head and sat quietly. By this time the congregation had assembled. The boys continued walking among them with the censers burning and the girls were all lined up to the right of the altar. The high priest removed the goat's head and placed it on the altar. He then began the mass by holding the upside-down cross in his right hand and making the sign of the cross with his left. The congregation also used their left hand to make this sign and they all repeated aloud, "Ghost Holy the and Son the and Father the of name the in." They then repeated the Lord's Prayer backwards with the exception of the opening line where they said, "Our Father which art on earth."

By the time they had repeated the litany and several prayers backwards a dull opium cloud hung over the congregation. It was obviously having its effect as the men howled, screamed, and made loud animal noises while dancing wildly. Amelia began feeling the effect too. A cloud closed in on her and, though she struggled to stay alert, she was being wrapped in a blanket of apathy. Her eyes were heavy and her body felt like lead.

Matthew grabbed Amelia's arm and whispered, "Amelia!"

Amelia was still in a haze and her response was barely audible. "I'm just so tired of trying. I don't want anymore trying," she said as her head drooped to Matthew's shoulder.

A moment later the high priest raised his arms over his head and the congregation sat back in their seats. Some fell off the benches and struggled to get up. When they were all seated the head priest walked around the altar and down to where the two circles were on the floor.

Without a word from the priest, the four girls followed him and stood just outside the circles. First he took the five-sided star from one of the pillows and stepped into the middle of the center circle placing the star on the floor. Then the other three girls leaned forward holding their pillows out to him.

Next the priest took the ebony handled dagger and put it in a black leather belt that he wore around his waist. Then he took the sword in his right hand and the wand in his left. The girls all moved simultaneously back to the altar as the priest held his wand and sword over his head.

He began chanting, "I conjure and command thee, O Cernunnos, by Paumachie, Baldachienses, Apolorodedes and the most powerful Princes Genio and Liachide, Ministers of the Seat of Tartarus and Chief Princes of the Throne of Apologia in the ninth region; by Him who spoke and it was done; by the most Holy and Glorious names Adonai, El Elohim, Elohe, Zabaoth and Tetragrammaton, appear forthwith and show thyself to me, here outside this circle, in fair and human shape, without horror or deformity and without delay. Speak to me visibly, clearly and without deceit. Possess my mind and my body. Answer all my demands and perform all I desire. Do not linger. The King of Kings commands thee."

Immediately the priest went into a deep trance with his chin dropping to his chest. A minute later his head jerked up, his eyes opened wide, and he stepped outside of both circles without touching either one. Next, two men joined him at the altar. One man handed the priest some type of chalk and he proceeded to draw a triangle on the floor. Then the other man put evergreen boughs around the outside of the triangle along with some skulls from horned animals. As the men did this the congregation chanted over and over, "Thunor, Balor, Ares, Mars."

Finally, the priest took a drink of wine and then sprinkled it over the triangle while saying, "Eko, Eko, Azarak." His voice sounded completely different. In the meantime one man had ground up some herbs and powder with the mortar and pestle and now he handed it to the priest who placed it in the triangle.

He yelled out, "I work to the destruction of Amelia Noel. I work to the destruction of Amelia Noel." Then he took a chunk of clay and began molding it while saying Amelia's name over and over again.

Amelia clung to Matthew's arm and said silently, "They're trying to kill me!" When the priest finished he engraved something into the doll and chanted, "In the name of Cernunnos, the War God of Mars, and the spirit of destruction and revenge, Cernunnos, the Horned One, creature of clay, I name thee Amelia Noel."

He then took the doll and placed it at the tip of the triangle. Next, using a scarlet candle, he dripped wax around the triangle and began chanting the most horrible descriptions of destruction, revenge and malice which were all aimed at Amelia. He described how he wanted her to suffer and die and then repeated it over and over again. Finally, he stood at the tip of the triangle and crossed his arms over his chest while chanting, "It is not my hand which does this deed but that of Cernunnos, the Horned One."

He then took a long needle in his left hand and began chanting, "Arator, Lapidator, Omtator! Somniator, Subaerfor, Iquator!   Signator, Sudator, Combustor! Comestor, Onerator!" Then he viciously stabbed the doll with the needle and yelled, "So mote it be!"

Amelia felt a sharp, burning pain and knew she was dying.

Chapter XIV

What could you want
that Forgiveness cannot give you?

Amelia felt herself being pulled away from her body and then she hovered about ten feet above everybody else. She could see all the people in the temple including herself lying in Matthew's arms. Then she continued moving up, right through the ceiling of the temple and up through the earth. Swiftly she flew above everything and moved out of the atmosphere. She found herself drawn through an energetic vortex and into a world she'd never imagined.

Her mind had perfect clarity. Her body felt light, nearly transparent, and her senses were totally alive. Everything was so vivid. It was as if she'd spent her life seeing through dark glasses, wearing heavy boots and layers of clothing. And for the first time she was feeling warm sand under her feet and a delicious tropical breeze on her skin before diving naked into a warm, crystal clear lake.

Without question, Amelia knew this was death and she was finally home. Standing before her was a beautiful, angelic man. Light radiated from his entire being, yet he definitely had physical features. He was tall with sandy colored, curly hair, full lips and blue eyes even more intense than the blue in Äsha's eyes. He communicated with such richness; no language could ever embrace the depth of feeling he was able to impart.

Amelia traveled with him. She learned that although there are many "realities" created for learning purposes, there was one reality that remained constant, unchanging, called Prime Reality. "God" was known as Prime Creator or, more simply, Love.

She was shown the most amazing overview of her life and life on earth. She could see acts of kindness, love and courage as sparks of light shooting up from the planet, as well as fear, anger and hatred in the form of dark patches. Tears came to her eyes when she saw there was much more light than darkness, so many more acts of love than hate.

There was perfect sense to everything. She saw that everything was a choice between love and fear and every choice that each person made was the perfect learning experience for him. No matter what, every single person on the planet was in a constant state of learning. If they chose to learn through fear, the lessons were painful; if they chose to learn through love, they'd experience joy.

Judgment didn't exist except in the minds of those believing themselves to be guilty. She saw that in prime-reality everything was about learning, but how an individual learned or the amount of "time" involved was of no consequence. If a person was in kindergarten, they were in kindergarten and it didn't matter if they repeated kindergarten over and over; it was their choice.

Children of Light

Even though she left her physical body behind, Amelia could see for herself there was no death. What was called birth and death was more like a revolving door, much more of an entrance than an exit.

In Prime Reality, she saw no one could ever be harmed and there was nothing to fear . . . in the same way that one could never really be harmed in a dream. What seemed painful was only because fear had been chosen, and that in itself was a marvelous learning experience, giving each one the opportunity to make a different choice the next time. At some point learning through fear and pain would cease to have an appeal.

Amelia was shown that, at best, suicide is futile and the people who tried it found they had to go back and start all over again. What made it particularly painful was that those who chose suicide were shown how that choice affected others. Amelia watched as a man who had committed suicide physically felt his mother's feelings of anguish over the loss of her son. He felt his wife and children's feelings, too, and saw how his suicide would indelibly affect their lives. It wasn't punishment or retribution; it was a means to learn. Everyone had the opportunity to learn by experiencing how they affected others during their lifetime on earth. They saw the "ripple effect" of everything they said or thought, for positive or negative. Then they judged for themselves whether or not they had accomplished their "mission."

Amelia was surprised to see that the *only* things that really "counted" on earth were choices for love. Fear was an easy choice. Painful, yes, but nonetheless familiar. Fame and fortune didn't matter in the least. The ones who really progressed were those who were loving; they were the ones who got to graduate and move on. They could be on any dimension and go anywhere in the universe. They could even materialize on a street corner in New York City, do a good deed, and disappear!

Finally, her guide took Amelia back to the temple. As she looked down, it all seemed so unreal, so dreamlike. The guide said to her, "You don't have to work to overcome darkness. It doesn't exist. There's no darkness so powerful, so intense, that it isn't instantly dispelled by even the smallest amount of light. You don't need a lot of knowledge or training, Amelia. All you need is an open heart with the desire to love. If you embrace every experience as an opportunity to learn, then pain and joy, suffering and ecstasy, become one. You'll throw your arms in the air and yell, 'Thank you! Thank you! Thank you! I love learning!'"

Amelia felt the most incredible wave of love through her body.

"It's time for you to return," said her guide. "Remember, you're seeing people who've forgotten who they are and where they've come from.

"But *this* is my home!" cried Amelia. "Can't I stay here with you?"

"In your case," he said smiling, "do you know what 'HOME' stands for?"

Amelia shook her head.

"'Heaven On Mother Earth.' That's your mission; that's what you're there to accomplish," he said.

"But how can I do that?" said Amelia.

"Feel Love!"

"That's it?!"

"Think about it. When you *feel* love, is it possible to be angry, resentful, hateful? You can't feel love and fear at the same time; you're always choosing one or the other. If you feel love, then you're automatically forgiving. Is there anything you want that forgiveness can't give you? Forgiveness isn't just about others; it's a gift you give yourself. It's the understanding that you don't know everything and the decision that you won't judge. Everyone can see life in terms of lessons being learned but judgment is your decision that someone isn't learning fast enough. It's saying 'I'm right and you're wrong and you deserve to suffer for not doing things my way.' My dear, if people knew a better way they'd take it. If they're in darkness, they need light, not judgment. How others choose to learn is none of your business. If you bring light into the prison cell and the inmates close their eyes, it's not your concern."

"But I've been with these people. They're incredibly powerful. I don't know enough to fight them."

"No, Amelia. If you fight darkness you make it real. You need a different perspective. Think of the darkest, most frightening Halloween funhouse you can imagine. The building is only one story high but it's filled with mazes and booby traps and 'things that go bump in the night!' And let's say that you have to walk through the entire place in pitch blackness just feeling your way along. The people in their costumes know when you're coming; they can even hear your heart beating. They're not frightened; they're in their element. But would you be frightened?"

"I have no doubt!" said Amelia.

"Now, if instead, the roof were removed from the building in broad daylight and you could see the layout with all the actors and the props, would you still be frightened?"

"No," she said, laughing.

"It's all a matter of perspective. "If you focus on darkness, there you'll be; or you can simply turn on the light! Stay in your element, Amelia! How can darkness do battle with light? It can't even show up! No matter what's happening, you can always choose love. There's nothing chaotic in the universe; there's wisdom behind everything."

The next thing Amelia knew she was waking up in Matthew's arms.

Matthew held her tightly and whispered, "Oh, my God, Amelia! I thought you were dead!"

At that moment the head priest was standing behind the altar and he cried out, "Cernunnos, Cernunnos! To you I sacrifice the blood of innocence. I give you the blood of life for the blood of my enemy's life!" Still in a trance, the girl wearing the snake necklace walked stiffly up to the stone altar. The priest picked her up and reverently laid her on the sacrificial table. He pulled out his ebony-handled dagger and chanted, "This blood sacrifice is the atonement between man and Prince Lucifer. We shall be ONE with the night!"

As the priest raised the dagger over his head Amelia whispered to Matthew, "Remember the night we danced together? Close your eyes and *feel* that love."

Matthew looked at her skeptically for a moment.

She said quickly, "Trust me! Dance in your heart! Imagine that girl dancing in her own heart and see that man in bright, golden light."

Matthew held Amelia in his arms as they closed their eyes and felt love in their hearts. Amelia felt love flowing inside herself and radiating out. She felt absolutely no fear. As she opened her eyes the head priest dropped to the floor and began writhing in convulsions. He screamed and yelled in agony as men from the congregation rushed to his aid.

Immediately all of the kids regained their normal consciousness. The girl on the altar sat up and in the commotion she and the others hurried up the aisle toward the exit totally unnoticed.

When they reached them, Amelia threw off the cloak and Matthew took off his animal mask. Before anyone could speak, Amelia put her finger to her lips and motioned for everyone to follow her. She led them up the spiral stairway through the secret door and into the hall.

Amelia said, "Matthew, will you take everyone to find the others? Hopefully all of the guards are in the temple. I'll meet all of you at the main entrance."

Matthew said, "What about you? Where are you going?"

"I still have some things to do. I can't explain now."

Amelia raced down the hall heading back toward the laboratory with the animals. Just before reaching the lab she heard a man walking heavily and quickly toward her. There were no doorways but there was a metal grid in the wall with a knob on the bottom. She gave it a hard pull and it noiselessly swung open. She climbed into a large air duct and pulled the grid closed.

A moment later a man walked briskly down the corridor and stopped in front of the air duct where Amelia was hiding.

He said sternly, "Amelia, enough fun and games. I know you're in there and you won't like it if I have to come and get you."

Amelia sat quietly, barely breathing. The man continued with a more soothing voice, "My dear, don't you realize I know all about you? I know your thoughts. I hear you talking to Matthew. I've seen you walk through walls and, I must say, that's quite clever. And your diversion technique in the temple was indeed remarkable for a mere child."

Amelia didn't move.

"I see you're still not convinced. Well, I know all about your silly little friend Äsha and all the ridiculous things she taught you. How love and goodness are supposed to be *so powerful* and evil is helpless. You know so little!"

The man laughed wickedly and burning hot air blew through the duct. The metal became so hot that

Amelia could no longer stand it. The flesh on her hands burned as she crawled up to the grid. It flew open by itself and she climbed out.

The man was average in height and weight, with brown hair, but there was something frightening about his eyes. The iris was such a pale blue that it almost blended in with the white of his eyes and the pupil was no bigger than a pin point.

He affected a tone of mock pity, "It's too bad you can't practice what you preach. My dear, there was no heat in that metal. I simply made a suggestion to your pitifully weak mind and you were burned by your own fear."

Amelia looked down at her hands. They were swollen with painful blisters.

"Your silly mind games are no match for me! Every time you feel the pain in your hands you'll know who has the power. However, I don't want you to suffer. I'm not a cruel person. I'll take all the pain away if you join me."

Amelia's hands were so excruciatingly painful that she felt waves of unconsciousness flooding her mind. The room began to spin and the man's voice sounded far away. She struggled to break through the oppressiveness around her and said, "I'm not here to fight you or join you."

"Amelia, you will either join me or you'll have to fight me. Obviously, though, you're still not convinced." He half-smiled and yelled, "Guards!" Two guards ran toward them from another corridor and took Amelia's arms.

They led her down the hall and into a huge, bare room with no windows. At the far end of the room she saw Matthew sitting in a glass booth. The guards took her to the booth, shoved her inside and locked the door.

Along with the pain in her hands, Amelia had developed a serious migraine headache. She'd lost her peripheral vision. The left side of her body was going numb and she could barely formulate words.

Matthew noticed Amelia's hands, "My God, Amelia! What have they done to you?"

Amelia shook her head.

"What?"

"Shh," said Amelia, tapping her head.

Matthew could see that Amelia was in terrible pain so he just held her in his arms. Amelia relaxed a little and focused on a technique her mother taught her for getting rid of migraine headaches. She decided she may as well include her hands in the technique as well. First, she identified where the pain was located. She thought, "Both of my hands, the left side of my body, my temples, across my forehead." Next, she rated the pain on a scale of 1 to 10. She thought, "Ten. All the way around." Finally, she said to herself, "I'm willing to let this pain go."

The first time Amelia tried this technique she said it out loud to her mother. When she went to identify the location and intensity of the pain after repeating it once, she'd said, "It's the same."

Her mother said, "That's drawing on the past. Stay 'present.' Identify where it is and the intensity right *now*."

Amelia thought it was sort of silly at the time but then she noticed the "pain" started to move around, the intensity jumped up and down. Then it was gone. She looked at her mother incredulously and said, "Does this always work?"

"Every time," said her mother, nodding. "The only time it doesn't work is when someone quits trying."

The first time it took less than 15 minutes but now she had it down to five minutes or less. Amelia realized how much she loved her mother and how many things she'd learned from her.

As she went over the steps in her mind, Amelia started blaming herself for the painful blisters on her hands. The Critic said, "I told you to get a grip! You're not smart enough or strong enough to take these people on. You'll be ground up hamburger meat when they're done with you; those blisters will be nothing!"

In her mind Amelia said, "Thank you. Next!" She took a deep breath and started laughing, which seemed an odd response considering the situation. Fortunately, Matthew thought she was starting to cry so she didn't have to explain herself. Laughing during a tragic moment is generally frowned upon and Amelia's head still hurt too much to go into detail.

"Now what?" she said silently to herself.

Matthew said, "Are you asking me?"

Amelia looked at Matthew and laughed. "Actually," she said out loud, "I was talking to myself."

"Oh, sorry to interrupt!" he said, trying to keep a straight face. "I have a strange thing to tell you."

"What?"

He looked around cautiously and said, "Have you noticed that this little room we're sitting in is starting to fill up?"

"Fill up?"

"Look around. Can't you see shimmery light? Surely you can feel something?"

"I can feel something, but what is it?"

"Don't laugh. Well, it's okay if you do laugh. They like laughter," said Matthew.

"Who?"

"The angels." Amelia laughed and noticed that her headache was gone. However, before she could say anything else, the man with the pale eyes spoke to them over the loudspeaker. "My little friends, it would seem that you're both caught in an evil web that even your little fairy godmother can't get you out of. You have both made fools of my weak-minded staff but now you're dealing with me."

"Amelia's hands are but a small example of what I can do. I will now demonstrate that evil is the only power and you will both witness it's force. And just to show you that I'm a good sport, I will demonstrate this power with one of my own instructors."

The blondish-grey haired man that Matthew had seen teaching the class stepped into the room. He walked about fifty feet away and then squarely faced the pale-eyed man. Fear and hatred that permeated the room.

They could see energy around both men. The energy bubbled black and red with the heat and intensity of lava. The men aimed this energy at each other. Amelia and Matthew watched in horror as the blonde man began to shake uncontrollably. His breathing was hard and fast and he dropped to the floor writhing in convulsions. There was some sort of energetic barrier around each man but the barrier around the blonde man split open and the burning hot, black/red energy from the other man shot into his body.

The instructor blew apart from spontaneous combustion.

The force of the explosion shattered the glass booth and Matthew was knocked unconscious. The man with the pale eyes headed straight for Amelia. She could feel his thoughts of hatred trying to destroy her.

His wicked laughter echoed in the room. "You thought your little bit of training could save you? You stupid girl. You know nothing of POWER. All your thoughts about sweetness and light can't save you now! Go ahead, fight me!"

Amelia could feel her hands burning more painfully than ever as if they were actually on fire. She closed her eyes, took a deep breath, and heard the word, "SING!"

She sang as loud as she could. She didn't even know what she was singing but she was carried away by the song. She paid absolutely no attention to the man; it was as if he no longer existed. In that moment Matthew regained consciousness. He saw the most beautiful gold light filling the booth. Outside, the man with the pale eyes projected all of the black/red energy at them. The negative energy hit the gold light and was instantly mirrored back at the man; he was hit squarely between the eyes.

He screamed out in excruciating pain as he threw his hands over his eyes and dropped to his knees.

"I'm Blind!" he screamed. "Somebody help me. I can't see!"

He flailed his arms madly, groping in the dark. Still screaming in pain he crawled helplessly along the floor until he reached the broken glass from the booth. He yelled, "Get those God-damned kids!"

Matthew said, "Let's go!"

He stopped himself just before grabbing Amelia's hand and then noticed her hands were perfectly normal. Amelia looked at her hands and back at Matthew.

She smiled broadly and said, "Right! Let's go!"

As they walked out of the room Amelia looked at the man sitting helplessly on the floor. He was rocking back and forth whimpering, "Where is everybody? Somebody help me!"

Children of Light

They walked out the door and right past two guards who never saw or heard them. They took the elevator down to the cells. Matthew tried to remember the code but his mind went blank.

He turned to Amelia. "I'm afraid I don't know the code. There's no way to get everyone out without it."

Amelia said, "Don't concentrate. Just allow."

Matthew took a deep breath, punched in the code, and the door opened automatically. They turned on the lights, grabbed a set of keys, and quickly released everybody. They had difficulty seeing in the bright lights so Matthew and Amelia helped everyone out into the hall.

Matthew said, "Listen everyone! For some reason I can't explain nobody can see us at the moment." Little whispers and gasps escaped the group. Matthew continued, "Just stay calm. Don't be afraid. Try not to panic if you see guards."

Amazingly enough, everyone seemed quite calm under the circumstances. They walked quietly and cautiously, close to the wall. They were almost to the elevator when they heard the sound of several men walking briskly down a different corridor. There was no place to hide so they pressed themselves up against the wall, hoping the men would walk by without looking.

Amelia closed her eyes and saw Timothy. Bits and pieces of her conversation with him raced through her mind. "This 99.9999% empty space, the Universal Consciousness, is actually full of intelligence, and because it isn't in form yet, it's full of potential. So you *are* that unlimited intelligence and you *are* that unlimited potential. But you must be conscious of this power to use it . . . . The only reason you 'can't' is because your belief, your conviction, that it's impossible is stronger than your belief that it is possible. Could you walk through that wall in your mind? You're *choosing* to see a wave *or* a particle: Mind *or* matter . . . . They're not separate entities; they're one. Things Are Thoughts! Impossibilities Never Occur!"

Then she thought of the cave in India and remembered Äsha explaining that the yogi was simply projecting images into the mind of the psychiatrist. Without a word she grabbed Matthew's arm and said silently, "See the entire group as invisible to the guards." They both closed their eyes and held this mental image. The guards turned the corner and walked directly down the hall toward them. Involuntarily one of the girls gasped and a guard looked directly at her without seeing a thing. Everyone in the group appeared shocked and confused but they remained silent as they got on the elevator and rode up to the main level.

No one noticed them as they made their way to the entrance. When they reached the door everyone stopped and stared. There was no way to open it. Apparently the door was controlled automatically in some other part of the building.

Everyone started talking at once.

"Oh, my God. There's no way out!"

"What are we going to do?"

"What good is it to get this far, if we can't get out?"

"Where are we gonna to go?"

"The guards are sure to spot us. We'll all be killed!"

The alarms went off and guards raced down the hall yelling, "There they are! At the exit!"

As shots rang out they realized they were at a dead end and utterly trapped.

Amelia yelled, "Everybody hold hands."

With the exception of Matthew, everyone looked at her like she was crazy. But as bullets ripped through the air and ricocheted around them she yelled forcefully, "**Do it!**" Frantically they grabbed each other's hands.

Amelia shot a mental picture to Matthew. The image was the cave in India when the psychiatrist had walked between the two cobras and was protected by an energetic force-field when the snakes tried to strike. Then she thought of Äsha's definition of fear: "false evidence appearing real." Matthew understood immediately and joined her in holding the image of a protective force-field around the entire group.

Though automatic weapons were being fired, a strange thing happened. It was silent. The gunfire seemed to have stopped, but then they noticed bullets hitting an energetic field and dropping harmlessly around them on the floor! Speechless, they all turned and stared at Matthew and Amelia.

Amelia felt a powerful energy surge through her body. There was a radiance emanating from her that everyone could see.

She said quietly, "Close your eyes. Matthew and I will take you through the door."

Guards were now running down the corridor and some of the students started to protest, yelling that it was impossible. So Amelia stepped through the door and reappeared moments later and said simply, "Impossibilities never occur. Now, will you all please close your eyes."

With Amelia at the front and Matthew at the end of the line they led everybody through the door and into the dark cavern beyond. On the other side they could hear the clink of bullets hitting the metal door.

"You can all open your eyes now," yelled Amelia. "Keep holding hands! We'll lead you out."

Amelia and Matthew could both see the same way they'd been able to see on that first night with Äsha. They walked as quickly as possible toward the cave entrance but it was difficult with everybody tripping and losing their balance in the dark. They were halfway to the entrance when the spotlights were switched on and the vault door swung open. Swarms of guards poured into the cavern with automatic weapons.

Suddenly, the cave vibrated and trembled under their feet. They heard a tremendous thundering from outside as rocks fell from the ceiling. When they reached the mouth of the cave they were shocked to see live volcanos spewing lava over the land. They were surrounded on all sides by whirling tornados closing in on them and an earthquake shook the land with such force that the cave collapsed behind them.

Children of Light

Amelia closed her eyes and shut out everything her senses were telling her. She remembered the high priest saying, "Cernunnos! To you I sacrifice the blood of innocence." It felt as if they were all victims about to be sacrificed to the elements. Amelia closed her eyes and remembered the vision at the bottom of the ocean. In her body she felt the dolphins and whales singing; she felt peace and the joy of seeing her friends "dancing" alive and well. She knew with all her heart that they were all perfectly safe; nothing could harm them. And she thought of the angelic man telling her that home was "Heaven On Mother Earth."

Matthew could feel Amelia's thoughts and feelings and he held the same feeling. Though there was hail the size of golf balls, fire shooting out of the earth and lightning striking within inches, they were untouched. The gale force wind around them didn't even blow their hair. The ground beneath their feet ripped apart and fire shot into the air engulfing the entire group.

None of them even felt a sensation of heat and all at once they rose gently above the earth. There was no sense of air pressure and everyone could breathe normally even though they had risen to the point where they could view the entire planet. Everyone was laughing and talking until they looked back and saw what was happening. The oceans had completely drained away and the entire earth was on fire. They could see the earth being sucked into itself at an unbelievable speed and, in a brilliant flash of light, it completely disappeared. All that was left was the blackness of outer space.

Chapter XV

Going H.O.M.E.

The next thing they knew, they were all sitting in the old, yellow bus heading for home. They were within a few miles of their high school and nowhere near where the bus had broken down. Everyone appeared dazed, as if awakened from some bizarre dream. Matthew was sitting next to Amelia and, as they looked at the others on the bus, he grabbed her arm and said, "Look!"

There sat Tom near the front of the bus. He looked as shocked and surprised as everyone else. In a few moments everyone began to laugh and talk normally as if nothing unusual had happened. Amelia and Matthew overheard a boy and girl talking in front of them. Jason, who had been one of the boys swinging a censer at the black mass, said, "I just had the strangest dream and you were in it, Emma. You were wearing some kind of a gold necklace; and then we were running through a cave out to some volcanos, or something like that." He paused for a moment and laughed. "It doesn't really make much sense anymore. My memory's so blurry."

Emma said, "You know, I think I had a weird dream too; I can't remember it though. Oh, well. That's typical. They never make much sense."

Amelia looked at Matthew and said directly to his thought, "They all think this was a dream! Why is it all so clear to us?"

Matthew took Amelia's hand and said, "This is clear to you? You mean to tell me you actually understand everything that's happened here?"

Amelia shook her head and said, "Well, no. I don't understand everything, but at least I can remember it all clearly."

Before she could say any more, Mrs. Caldwell stood up in the front of the bus. She glanced at her watch and said, "Listen up, everybody. It appears we'll be arriving about an hour ahead of schedule. So I'll unlock the side door at school and you can all take turns using the phone to call your parents. Before you do that, however, be sure you all have your gear out of the bus because it won't be there when you get back from your phone call. Thanks for a great trip everyone. We'll do it again next year!"

Everyone on the bus applauded and a moment later they pulled into the school parking lot. Amelia and Matthew found their backpacks on the overhead racks above them. Since they were sitting at the back of the bus, there was already a long line of kids waiting for the telephone.

Matthew said, "Amelia, I live just a few blocks from here. Would you like to walk home with me and use the phone at my house? Or I could just give you a ride home?"

Amelia smiled and said, "Thanks."

Going H.O.M.E.

As they walked to Matthew's house Amelia said, "I'm having a little trouble adjusting to the idea that we're somehow back to 'real life.'"

Matthew smiled, "What do you think that's gonna be like exactly? You and I are still telepathically connected. And we share a story so bizarre we'd be locked up for life if we ever told anyone."

"Well, hopefully they'll lock us up together," said Amelia with a wink.

"Do you realize we couldn't prove a single thing?" said Matthew.

"Well, would you rather be right or would you rather be happy?"

They both burst out laughing and Matthew put his arm around Amelia as they walked up the driveway to his house.

Amelia said, "You live here?!" It was a three story mansion set on ten acres of perfectly manicured lawn surrounded by elegant gardens.

Matthew nodded, "You'll remember this place from the cave. It was originally my grandparent's home. It's a little embarrassing living in such a pretentious house. People usually get the wrong idea. Come on in. You can meet 'My Parents,'" he said, raising his eyebrows mysteriously.

Amelia said, "Does this mean you're taking me on the guided tour?"

"Of course!" Matthew flung open the front door with a grand gesture and Amelia stepped into the house.

The front entryway was just as she remembered it. They set their packs down by the front door.

Matthew said, "I think we'll start off with the darkest, most depressing room, get it out of the way. I call it the Lion's Den since my dad has all of his safari conquests pegged to the wall. He had the room done in dark wood paneling. He always keeps it dark and gloomy to reflect his mood." Matthew opened the door to the den and said, "I don't believe it." The room was full of light. In place of wood paneling the walls were painted a soft peach with white molding. There were no animal heads or skins, no guns hanging on the walls. Instead, there were bouquets of flowers and delicate watercolor pictures. The room was decorated with beautiful white furniture and glass tables with a lovely pastel rug in the center of the room.

Amelia said, "This is it?"

"Apparently, Mother did some fast redecorating. Unbelievable!"

At that moment Mrs. McKinley entered the room smiling and said, "What's unbelievable?"

"Oh, hi, Mom!" Matthew quickly introduced Amelia to his mother and said, "I was wondering how you managed to redecorate this room so quickly."

She laughed and said, "What on earth are you talking about? This room hasn't been redecorated since you were ten years old."

Going H.O.M.E.

Matthew looked at Amelia, then back at his mother. He said, "Alright, then. Tell me where the safari animals are and all of Dad's guns?"

His mother paused for a moment, looked intently at Matthew and said, "Are you feeling alright?"

"Yeah," he replied, a bit confused. "Why?"

"Well, dear, you know your father has never touched a gun in his life. He can't bear to see an animal harmed. The only time your father ever shoots an animal is with a camera. Amelia, dear, come see what Matthew's father has done."

They walked into a long hallway that had windows on one side and was lined with gorgeous pictures of animals and wild flowers on the other. Mrs. McKinley said proudly, "Matthew's father took every one of these pictures. He's traveled all over the world and this year there's even going to be a wildlife calendar composed exclusively of his work."

Amelia said, "He's a wonderful artist!"

Matthew said silently to Amelia, "I've never seen these pictures in my life!"

They walked quietly down the hall, exchanging glances as Matthew's mother led them outside. Matthew's father was leaning over the garden when his wife waved and yelled, "Darling, look who's here!"

He straightened up with a bouquet of flowers in his hands and smiled broadly. With long, swift strides he headed toward them. As he got closer Amelia realized he looked years younger; nothing like the pale, sickly man she had seen in the cave. He was healthy with a glowing complexion and rosy cheeks like Matthew's.

His eyes sparkled as he hugged Matthew and said, "It's great to have you home!"

Matthew said, "Dad, this is my friend, Amelia."

Mr. McKinley smiled, handed her a beautiful yellow rose and said, "I'm delighted to meet you."

He then turned, handed his wife a bouquet of flowers and said sweetly, "And these are for you, darling."

She hugged him and said softly, "I love you so much."

Mr. McKinley winked at Amelia and said, "This is what it's like to be on a honeymoon for twenty-two years."

Amelia smiled and Matthew said, "I really should get Amelia home. It's been an awfully long trip."

They all said goodbye and as Amelia and Matthew headed back to the house she glanced over her shoulder and saw Matthew's parents strolling through the garden with their arms around each other. She said, "Your parents are really in love with each other."

Matthew shook his head slowly and said, "I don't understand. I've never heard him say a kind word to my mother, let alone pick flowers for her." He looked at Amelia intently and said, "My father has been sick for years. He was skinny and pale a few days ago. Now he weighs at least twenty pounds more. He's healthy and happy."

Going H.O.M.E.

Matthew grabbed Amelia's backpack, threw it into the back of his convertible and said, "Alright, let's see if there are any surprises at *your* house!"

They walked into Amelia's house and she yelled, "Dad, I'm home!"

Her mother pushed through the swinging door that led into the kitchen and said, "What? You don't say 'Hi' to your mother anymore?"

Amelia said, "Oh, hi, Mom. I just didn't expect you to be here."

Her mother laughed and said, "Well, I live here don't I? Where else would I be?"

Though she was puzzled, Amelia said, "Mom, this is Matthew."

"Hi, Matthew. Why don't you both come into the kitchen? I'm teaching Amelia's father how to make applesauce." She looked at Matthew, smiled and said, "We're an 'equal opportunity' household!"

They stepped into the kitchen and Amelia saw her father perched on top of a stool, wearing Mrs. Noel's frilly Christmas apron, while he pared apples. Amelia introduced Matthew.

Her father said with mock seriousness, "Alright, I don't want either of you laughing at my brush with domestication. I foolishly promised your mother that I'd do whatever she wanted for our twentieth anniversary and look what she has me doing! Ah, the cost of true love!"

Children of Light

Mrs. Noel stood behind her husband and wrapped her arms around him. She looked lovingly at him, kissed him on the cheek, and said, "What dedication!"

Amelia laughed and said, "Dad, are you going to let us sample the finished product a little later?"

Her father said, "Sure. This should be done in about half an hour. In the meantime, why don't you take Matthew down to see the pond?"

Matthew and Amelia walked behind the house and sat on a small hill above the pond. Weeping willows dotted the edges and a small waterfall was at one end. There were all different kinds of ducks and birds along with a variety of small animals. Amelia said, "I think these animals must be migrating; I've never seen so many here before. She looked sadly at the animals and said, "I know that in light of what's happened this sounds trivial, but I had an experience I never had the chance to tell you about."

Matthew said, "You're talking about the lab, aren't you? I saw what you went through. It's not trivial to feel badly about those animals. I understand exactly how you feel."

Matthew put his arm around Amelia and said, "You know how you used to get mad at the way that I understood things before you did? Well this time I don't have any idea what's happened. I mean, one minute we're watching the earth self-destruct and the next minute we're home, but everything's changed." He laughed and said, "Like our old pal Äsha used to say, 'Everything will be the same, and everything will be different.'"

Amelia smiled and said, "I wish Äsha were here. She could explain all of this."

From behind them came a familiar voice. "Äsha? Why Äsha? What about the rest of us?!" It was Timothy and he was sitting in a semicircle with Äsha, Anna and Marie. Amelia and Matthew turned and hugged them.

"I can't believe you're all here!" exclaimed Amelia.

"Well, why not?" replied Timothy.

"Because you're all from a different dimension."

"Not any more," said Timothy.

Puzzled, Amelia said, "What do you mean?"

All of a sudden she noticed light emanating from everyone, including herself and Matthew. She looked around and saw light everywhere. There was a soft glow around plants, trees, flowers. Everything was glowing. And then she realized she could hear music and it was coming from a small stone.

She looked at the stone and burst out laughing. Hearing her thoughts, Matthew picked up the little stone and listened. He heard, "Hmm, Hmm, hmm, hmm."

He laughed, "Amelia, it's humming!"

"I know!" she said with delight. "Oh, look!"

On top of the stone was a tiny fairy, dancing while the stone was humming.

Smiling, Anna said, "My dear children, your planet is no longer on the third dimension. You've moved into a higher dimensional vibration. Your eyes are now open to see the miracles of creation that have been here all along!"

"You mean we've always had dancing fairies and humming stones?" asked Amelia.

"Ah, yes. Of course," replied Anna. "And much more than that."

"Why didn't I see this a few minutes ago before all of you joined us?"

"Because you didn't believe it was possible. And now you do!" chimed in Marie.

"How did this happen?" asked Matthew.

"You remember the monkeys on the island of Koshima? Critical mass?" replied Äsha. "Your **conscious choice** to see beyond the illusion caused a self-sustaining chain reaction for the entire planet."

"But what happened to the earth?" said Amelia.

"The earth as you knew it no longer exists," said Timothy.

"It wasn't real in the first place! Don't forget, it was all an illusion. You just decided to wake up from the dream," said Marie.

"We did?" said Amelia.

"When the two of you decided to redefine 'home' as 'heaven on mother earth,'" said Timothy, "those elements of fear and hatred, typical of the third dimension, could no longer coexist with your mental conviction. Remember, whatever you focus on becomes your reality!"

"But our families are completely different!" exclaimed Matthew. "We both have a history that never existed before!"

"Matthew," said Marie, "Could you wake up from a dream and discover that in reality you have a completely different 'history'?"

"Yes."

"Everything is pure consciousness!" continued Marie. "Nothing's impossible in your mind. Everything is pure **potentiality**. What the two of you chose to believe became out-pictured as your experience."

Äsha said, "Remember when we talked about the difference between 'hoping' and 'knowing'? To know an outcome means you already see it as fact. The power of your own intention to see beyond the illusion of the third dimension caused it to disappear. Amelia, you remember learning how to be unafraid and turn your nightmare-monsters into a piece of cheese and then you stopped having nightmares altogether? Quite simply, you did the same thing by focusing beyond the stormy seas of the third dimensional nightmare and you saw and felt an invisible world. And that world is now your reality."

Amelia said, "Äsha, I still feel badly that I wasn't able to save those little animals."

Äsha smiled sweetly and said, "Nothing good is ever destroyed."

At that moment Amelia felt something furry crawl into her lap. The baby rabbit she'd held in the lab nuzzled her hand. With tears in her eyes she looked up, but they'd all vanished.

She laughed and said to Matthew, "I can't believe the way these people come and go!"

Amelia's father yelled from the back door, "Is anybody interested in some fresh, HOME-made applesauce?"

She yelled back, "We'll be right there."

Amelia carefully sat the baby rabbit on the ground. She turned to Matthew and said, "For the first time in my life I feel like I'm really home."

Matthew held both of Amelia's hands, looked directly into her eyes, and said, "We'll never leave Kansas again, Dorothy!"

He then scooped up the bunny in one hand and said, "Come on, Toto! Let's go home!"

With their arms around each other, they walked up the hill following the fragrance of "HOME-made" applesauce!

To the Night

Have come the Dancers

Stars from the Heavens

Light on Earth

Seekers of the Searchers

Gently leading them

Home

.

Additional Reading

A Return to Love, Marianne Williamson

Chicken Soup for the Soul, Jack Canfield, Mark Victor Hansen, eds.

Quantum Healing, Deepak Chopra, M.D.

Empowerment, John Randolf Price

Bringers of the Dawn, Marciniak

E.T. 101, Diana Luppi

Celestine Prophecy, James Redfield

Mutant Message Downunder, Marlo Morgan

Emmanuel's Book (I, II, & III) P. Rodegast & J. Stanton

Illusions, Richard Bach

Way of the Peaceful Warrior, Dan Millman

A Guide for the Advanced Soul, S. Hayward

Feelings Buried Alive Never Die, K. Truman

Secrets of the I Ching, Joseph Murphy

Autobiography of a Yogi, Paramahansa Yogananda

The Hundredth Monkey, Ken Keyes

Be Here Now, Ram Dass

You Can Heal Your Life, Louise Hay

Inner Child Cards, Lerner & Lerner

Books or tapes about Neurolinguistic Programming

A Course in Miracles, or books based on the Course

The How To Book of Teen Self Discovery, and Freeze Frame, both by Doc Lew Childre

ACKNOWLEDGMENTS

The person to whom I owe the deepest debt of gratitude is Dr. Ted Conger, who has given me moral support and financial assistance in creating this book and tapes series. I'd also like to acknowledge his humanitarian efforts in feeding Utah's homeless and hungry.

To Al Robbs and to Janine Groth for their faith and commitment to the vision of this project.

To Dr. Enrico Melson for so lovingly donating his time and energy to this project and for the incredible depth and wisdom he so willingly shares with others.

To Ram Dass for inviting me to join a seven-day retreat, which helped me to bring my vision into reality.

To Deepak Chopra, Marianne Williamson, and John Randolf Price for their books and tapes that greatly influenced the writing of this book and to Madeleine L'Engle for her support and encouragement with my first draft.

To all of the people who played a role in bringing "Children of Light" into the public eye, including Maria Duncan, Michael Harris, Julia Lewis, Jim Morris, Jerry Schoening, Crystal Springs, Ed Sweeney, and Nancy and Bob Whittlesey.

To Robin Miller for giving me permission to use music from his four albums in the "Children of Light" tape series, and to Nyk Fry for his musical contribution and recording studio expertise.

To Denny Johnson for teaching the "heart dance," and

To Mel Larew for his friendship, legal advice and editing and layout efforts.